Praise for the novels of Curtis White

"White's work has a surrealistic, hallucinatory quality. More specifically, it's absurdist in the tradition of William Burroughs, Joseph Heller, and Terry Southern."

—Harvey Pekar, *The Austin Chronicle*

"White is a mischievous and omnivorous griot for the digital age . . . White wants readers to take stock of the timbre, texture and content of our times, and to ask, 'What have we learned? What have we lost?'" —Donna Seaman, *The Chicago Tribune*

"Witheringly smart, grotesquely funny . . . so moving as to be wrenching." —David Foster Wallace

"Curtis White writes out of an admirable intellectual sophistication combined with viscerality, pain, and humor." —John Barth

"Curtis White's fiction presents a scintillant, ironic surface, one that is barely able to contain the bleakness of American fin-de-siècle exhaustion, which latter is his essential theme."

—Gilbert Sorrentino

Lacking Character

Lacking
CHARACTER

a novel

Curtis White

MELVILLE HOUSE
BROOKLYN · LONDON

First Melville House Printing: March 2018

Melville House Publishing
46 John Street
Brooklyn, NY 11201
and
8 Blackstock Mews
Islington
London N4 2BT

mhpbooks.com
facebook.com/mhpbooks
@melvillehouse

Library of Congress Cataloging-in-Publication Data

Names: White, Curtis, 1951- author.
Title: Lacking character / Curtis White.
Description: Brooklyn : Melville House, [2018]
Identifiers: LCCN 2017045497 (print) | LCCN 2017051527
(ebook) | ISBN
    9781612196794 (reflow able) | ISBN 9781612196787 (softcover)
Subjects: LCSH: City and town life--Fiction. | BISAC:
FICTION / Humorous. |
    FICTION / Literary. | GSAFD: Humorous fiction.
Classification: LCC PS3573.H4575 (ebook) | LCC PS3573.
H4575 L33 2018 (print)
    | DDC 813/.54--dc23

LC record available at https://lccn.loc.gov/2017045497

ISBN: 978-1-61219-678-7
ISBN: 978-1-61219-735-7 (library edition)
ISBN: 978-1-61219-679-4 (eBook)

Design by Betty Lew

Printed in the United States of America

10   9   8   7   6   5   4   3   2   1

For Nicolas

Lacking Character

1.

—after E.T.A. Hoffmann

What follows is a story of contagion, and it begins, as all such stories must, with a message both obscure and appalling.

The city in which this message was passed was the city of N— in the geographic center of Illinois, and, as the saying goes, in the middle of nowhere. N— was notable as a place that had succeeded in achieving the destiny American cities had sought for centuries: complete abstraction. As the German mystic Jacob Boehme once observed, "It is not philosophers who are abstract, it is the man in the street." Actually, this story with its embedded message happened at least three times, in various places, but on the same spring date, as if this world were only a quarrelsome device like one of those old brightly painted tin toys that you'd wind up and watch as a dog jumped on a wagon and back, on a wagon and back, in that false infinity provided by winding a spring tightly.

The first time it happened was in 1810, in Dresden, as later attested to in a most remarkably vivid account by the gnomish writer of realist fantasy E.T.A. Hoffmann, in his story "Mademoiselle de Scuderi." Then it all fell out again in 1910, in Paris, on the edge of the first modern war. Picasso and Braques were hanging out, drinking yellow-green absinthe, and then enjoying hallucinations at that new sensation, the *Bijou*, the florid cinema. While they enjoyed such bohemian pleasures, the second coming of these remarkable events lit the air around their heads, the most brilliant heads of a most brilliant time, but, sadly, not even they noticed. They were painters, after all, and perhaps not open to the "unfolding" of things across vast stretches of time. That I know of, there is no record of the events happening elsewhere either (although I once imagined, wrongly as it turned out, that there were cryptic allusions to them in Franz Kafka's story "The Warden of the Tomb"). The third time that this story unfolded itself, as if the very air could open up like a Chinese paper box, was in 2010. Then, the residents of one house in N— were awakened from that self-satisfied sleep of the Midwest by a mad pounding at the door.

As it happened, all the women of the house were away sex-touring and ganja-smoking in Jamaica. The men had been left behind with strict instructions to lock the doors and ignore the baying of hounds. The men wondered if this pounding at the door was what the women meant by "the baying of hounds," so they went cautiously to an upstairs window.

"Open the door, for God's sake, open the door," a man's voice said, rising up above the sublime pounding he was giving to the door.

"Who is down there?" the men asked. "We know better than that, Mister. We were warned not to open the door to strangers."

"I must speak to the Marquis!"

"The Marquis? I think you have the wrong house. Try that big one at the end of the block."

"For God's sake, it's a matter of life and death. I stand falsely accused . . . of an atrocity."

"Well, why didn't you say so?!"

And down they went and unbolted the great oak portal.

No sooner had they opened the door than a figure wrapped in a flowing black cloak burst through violently, eyes wild, a man with the intensity of a demon!

"It's no wonder that you've been accused of an atrocity. Just look at yourself!"

The men now thoroughly regretted opening the door. One of them said, "Why don't you come back tomorrow at a decent hour?"

"Does destiny care for the time of day?" the man in the black garb asked.

They had no opinion on the matter.

"Why, then, if you won't take me, take this, and give it to the Marquis."

And he held an envelope aloft.

2.

"Childe Harold bask'd him in the noon–tide sun,
Disporting there like any other fly . . . "

—BYRON

When I try to picture him, the caped stranger looks a lot like Guy Williams in the old TV show "The Lives of Zorro," minus the mask. Oh, hell, let's give him a mask then. They're not expensive. You can get a bag of ten for a dollar-fifty at the Penury Factory Outlet down in Heyworth. So, if he wants a mask, *vamos!*, for God's sake. So, he's wearing a mask and one of those sexy flattop fedoras that I thought were simply the coolest thing in the world circa 1959. It even had a brightly wrought sterling silver band around it, if I'm not mistaken, although I might be thinking of Richard Boone's Paladin.

At any rate, this masked character at last got around to taking out an envelope in which was the note with the famous message he'd been promising.

"Take this letter to the Marquis. It is a matter of life and death—my death!"

One of them, let's call him Rory, stepped forward to say what all the others were thinking. "Sir," he said, "no offense, but this is not making a whole lot of sense to us. We have no idea who you are, there is no Marquis here—and, to tell you the truth, we're not collectively clear on just what a Marquis is—and you've frightened us a lot with your bizarre aspect. So, you might as well tell us what's in the envelope because we're just going to open it as soon as you leave."

The stranger looked perplexed, angry, frustrated. Perhaps he was a man with black belts in various martial arts, or a mob enforcer, perhaps he was Special Forces, a Navy SEAL, or someone with a lot of PTSD issues including the habit of savage resolution to situations that are not quite going his way. He waved the letter dramatically over his head—he was wearing really gorgeous black gloves, the softest calfskin, that went down his arm nearly to the elbow.

"I can tell you this: my letter comes from a woman of great power and influence living in a villa in the Hebrides. Have you never heard of the famous Queen of Spells? Surely, even in this depraved outpost of humanity, you have! I believe her letter touches on issues related to the flowing light of the Godhead. In this letter there is a vision of a great marble slab that lies at the base of a mighty mountain. There is a doorway in it like the doorway to a great city. A radiance as bright as that of the sun overflows the marble."

"Are you making this shit up?" asked one ruffian.

"Well, if that is not convincing to you, consider this," he said, and he turned and flung open the door.

The men looked out and saw that in the courtyard before their house hundreds, perhaps thousands, of Zorro-like guys were riding on small black horses—no more than two feet tall—rearing often and dramatically on their hind legs, as if the movie they were in was almost over and they were thinking about riding into the sunset. The men also waved envelopes—not Stetsons—high over their heads, messages galore. There they were in their pitchy vestments, as if the computer-graphics geeks had gotten carried away, gone a little haywire, in this scene. The men and horses roiled—anxious, trapped—and looked upon one another as if they were as terrified by this vision as were those who looked upon them. Stranger yet, they were crying great confused tears that flowed down their faces and seeped out beneath their little masks. But for what reason? That was what was so hard to say.

"This, *this*, is the reality that you scorn, on which you dare to look with your doubt and cynicism. Now, forthwith, to the Marquis!"

The men were overwhelmed by what they'd seen. They dropped their pretense and took the man directly to the Marquis.

3.

"We may lose more than 300 million people. So what? War is war. The years will pass and we'll get to work producing more babies than before."

—MAO

The men took the message to the Marquis in his chamber, the place where the critical issues of state were decided. The men said, "We are most sorry to disturb you, your Excellency, but this caped man has come on horseback to our door and insisted on delivering this message to you."

The Marquis looked up and said, "Well, it had better be important. I just achieved a new level in *Halo*."

"Really? You play *Halo*?"

He sighed.

"I play *Halo* to excess. Some days I think I am become *Halo*. Sometimes I can feel the numbers, the digits, flowing like fine sand in my head."

Although he was called the Marquis, he was usually just a regular guy, one of the boys, a dude, if you will. He liked to watch football on Sunday, and he was fond of racial slurs. He did all-nighters with his aristocrat pals over the Xbox. At his hands the aliens died in their legions. As for the business of state, it was often neglected. Of course, sad people lined up outside the Marquis's villa with sad faces and waited to petition him, but he rarely put in an appearance. Not because he didn't care, but because it took so long. "Seriously," he'd say, "those people have a *lot* of problems."

On the rare occasions when he did go outside to speak to his people, he usually ended up sitting on the curb with them and passing out little sandwiches and fruit juice. Invariably, he'd be so incensed by their unjust fates that he'd fire half his staff and spend days reforming the entire social and economic structure of his domain from the top down. Eventually, though, his longing for the game, the comfort he felt in the presence of the little aliens, would overcome him. He'd go back inside, and it would be months before he'd come back out. Only the pizza boys would be allowed in the courtyard. He'd re-hire the staff, and apologize to the industrialists he'd sent to jail, and promise not to interfere with their "important work" again. The people would simply return to being sad, which wasn't so bad, really; it seemed very natural for them. They were "good at it," as he said.

Strange as this may sound, he convinced himself that in killing these digital aliens in *Halo*, he *was* making an important contribution to the welfare of the people. At least it felt that way. At least he knew that his people did *not* have to worry about the sneaky little aliens. That problem he had put to rest, so sleep well, my people.

"What level are you going to?"

"I finally achieved the Heroic level."

"That's good," said Rory, "I've been beyond it, but that's pretty good." Rory served as the Marquis's amanuensis, so you'd think he'd know how sensitive his employer was about his virtual accomplishments.

The Marquis gave him what we used to call a dirty look, back in those forgotten days before emoticons when people exchanged facial expressions. If you're having trouble imagining what a dirty look was like, I can only assure you that this one was absolutely dirty, so dirty that Rory was frightened to look back at the Marquis and averted his gaze to a water-stained corner of the ceiling. Fortunately for Rory, while the Marquis wasn't used to trash talk, he was kind enough to "cut him slack," as humans once said, back when they actually said things.

"I may not be a *Halo* Legend," he intoned, looking down his noble nose, "but I am still the Marquis." Rory got the point.

"So you beat the parasitic Flood when it slipstreamed into New Mombasa and launched a melee?" he said, with desperate enthusiasm.

Another said, "That's like where the aliens capture a redoubt and the ugly, vicious things just start pouring forth . . . "

". . . like a replicating virus," said a staff member named Ted, who will now be retired from this narrative on a permanent basis. He's served his purpose, said his line, and now may leave.

"Wow, can you really handle that heavy stuff, your Illustriousness?" asked Rory. This used to be called "eating shit" back in the day, before our avatars did all the shit-eating for us, although once again you'll have to take my word for it.

The Marquis continued, meditating on something bizarre. He said, slowly, "Yes . . . replicating virus. A contagion. They did pour forth, you are quite right. But they weren't the usual sneaky aliens. Thousands of little men dressed in black and on horseback poured out from what looked like a large wicker clothes hamper that someone had abandoned in a backyard. They were dressed sort of like Zorro, if you remember him (of course you don't), or tiny versions thereof. Zorro was . . . never mind. The strangest thing was that they were *weeping*. They were milling around in confusion and bewilderment, not really attacking anything at all. Their weapons seemed to be little plastic swords. I thought something was wrong with the game, but once I started nailing them, that thought was beside the point. I took them down one after another. They gave out this little squeaky scream when they died. It was amazing and very satisfying." He grinned. "That's how I amassed points to become Heroic. Actually, it happened in just the last hour." In spite of what he was revealing, he seemed pleased with himself, as if he really had done something heroic.

"The one thing that surprised me was that each of the little men seemed to be subtly different from the others. It was as if, had I looked at one closely enough, I would have discovered a real individual little life there. I can't tell you what a charge that thought gave me as I slaughtered them. In fact, it even gave me an incipient hard-on. Sorry, I don't know how else to put it. What I mean by 'incipient' is that it was far from my Toro

Furioso, you know, with the veins black and twining about the thick neck of the beast. It was more just something between me and the little men. A sort of intimacy in death. A sort of softish thinking about being a hard-on but with no clear idea about why I'd need one just then. Do you know what I'm talking about? Well, why don't we agree, just among ourselves, to the idea that the little black men I slaughtered were individuated and that they caused me to have a hypothetical hard-on, a propositional, presumptive, or conjectural hard-on, a hard-on *in potentia,* as Aristotle would have put it."

The men exchanged awed looks. Everything they'd heard about the Marquis's acumen was true and then some. But the men also exchanged puzzled looks. They were veterans of the game, they'd camped out overnight in front of Best Buy the eve before every new release, and they knew that there was no framework or setting similar to what the Marquis had described. There was no atmosphere for the slaughter of little black Zorro characters on horseback or any other kind of back. But who among them had the guts to say so? It sure wasn't going to be Rory. He'd learned his lesson and the others had learned from him.

It was even worse for the masked man who'd followed them, who stood behind them now. He went pale at the thought of this slaughter. He had no idea what this game was, but he recognized the dead as his own tiny companions. The thought of the tide of death the Marquis described was disturbing to him in a deep way, as if the heated centers of his blood cells trembled.

Noticing him for the first time, the Marquis looked at the masked man and said, "And you, what may I do for you?" He paused, scrutinizing him. "Say, do I *know* you? You look familiar. You're not the whimsical fellow who lectured on Lord Byron's *Don Juan* last month at the Garrick Club, are you?"

The masked man was shattered. "I . . . I . . . what is a Garrick?"

"It's in London, for God's sake. Everyone knows that. The young scamp claimed to be from some dubious public university in North Dakota that's buried in snow nine months out of the year. And he wore a silly costume like you're wearing now. These youngsters and their cultural studies! Whatever happened to scholars, the sallow men in the bad sport coats? You know, the paunches, the nicotine stains on their fingers."

"What is London?"

"London!? You amaze me. You'd fit right in with that regalia. Carnaby Street would eat you up."

Tiring of his own badinage, the Marquis stretched forth his ermine-cuffed arm for the letter, snapping a finger impatiently. "Come, enough. Let's see this envelope of yours."

The Marquis tore open the letter and perused it for a moment, before turning it this way and that.

"What is this? It's nice stationery, handmade paper, if I'm not mistaken. But it's blank. Invisible ink or something?"

The masked man shrugged his shoulders. He had no clue. He was the bearer, not the author, of the letter. He felt as if he'd been captured in someone else's dream.

The Marquis continued, "Look, my friend, I bear you no ill will. I bear you no will at all. But I'm sure you know more than you're saying. See here, there is no need for cheese-paring with me."

Idiot inscrutability.

The Marquis scrutinized him anyway. I mean, he put his hand to his chin and studied him. Then, with a disappointed frown, he said, "My dear fellow, my very good sir, excuse me for saying so, but it seems to me that you look at things in just the way that people do."

Then for a moment they all froze as if in a *tableau vivant*, a sublimely blank moment. A certain cosmic (although I hate to use that fatuous word) process had engaged, and it snapped into place with the authority of some great mill wheel, yes, the mill wheel of the universe, and in that moment human consciousness stopped. The brave metaphysics that had for millennia made one thing different from all the other things came to a stop. The forces that had made stars different because now they were stars, and the forces that made the great variety of foodstuffs different because now they were foods, etc., all that stopped. Just for a moment, but I mean *stopped*. Everything in the room became undifferentiated mass, just mass, the Marquis flowing into Zorro, Zorro flowing into the threadbare Bokhara rug, the floor flowing up into night. But even this concedes too much to "looking at things in the way that people do." Clearly, there were no individual beings there, but it's not even clear that there was any being at all! The room was the place where everything and nothing were the same.

Perhaps it was something about the message, or something about bringing together the messenger and the Marquis. I can't say. But don't worry, it was just in that room, not everywhere, not in your neighborhood out in Anytown, USA, hub of every modern life, as you think. Happily, the Marquis's inner chamber soon returned, perhaps a little out of joint in some molecular way that you couldn't actually see.

At last, but this "at last" was after hardly a nanosecond, the Marquis said, "Did you guys just feel something, a kind of everything-at-once? And it's not the first time either. Doesn't last long, but it does blow my mind. Do you know that children's game, All Fall Down? Ashes! Ashes! It felt like that. As if we'd all suddenly succumbed to a disease. Or perhaps I should say that for a moment it felt like everything was everything else.

You know, like a child makes little critters out of clay and then mashes them all back into one big ball? Hmmm. I'm beginning to wonder about the quality of the hashish that the Eastern potentates have been bringing round of late. What kind of tribute is that, edgy hash? I'm tempted to send a squadron over to drop some shock and awe on them. See if they can figure out their *faux pas* and start sending me the good stuff again."

For your information, smoking hash while playing *Halo* was the best thing the Marquis knew about life. He called it his All-in-All. He didn't much like it when his All-in-All became an All-for-Naught. As for the shock and awe, he was making it up. He didn't even own a remote-controlled model airplane (if anyone remembers those in the age of the consumer drone) let alone a B-47. Actually, he was making it all up—the Garrick Club, the potentates, and especially the Toro Furioso. Only the threadbare carpet would hold up under investigation, and the hash, of course, but that's a basic, a necessity, a pantry essential.

Later, after the things of the world had returned to their rightful places and he was showing the men out, the Marquis asked Rory and the others over to play *Halo* on the next Tuesday. The Marquis would provide pizza and they'd bring the beer. "Only craft beers, now," he admonished, "and I'm still drinking stouts and porters. I know it's May, but it's been a cool spring, so I stick with the thick." He laughed at his own wordplay. "But I think we should give the hashish a rest, alas!"

Now the men were really seeing a plus-side to this weird evening. They were giddy with their good luck. They were going to play *Halo* with the Marquis at the Marquis's crib! And the funny Zorro man had made it all happen. They almost felt gratitude for the loser.

But they also thought that they'd got about as much out of him as they were going to, so they ushered him back out into the cobbled courtyard, eerily empty now of its cowboys. It was quiet except for that subtle echo of the receding past. As for the masked man, he was crushed by this experience. What was the meaning of his task? What should he make of what the Marquis had said? Where were his comrades on horseback? Had the Marquis really slaughtered them while playing some sort of game? And just who was he himself? He didn't even know that. A masked man, they said. Like someone named Zorro. Then he remembered: his name was Percy. But why Percy? Who gave him that name? Was there really a queen in the Hebrides? Was he just making it all up? And just what was he supposed to do next? He wanted to be a dutiful man, loyal to his task, but what was his duty and what his task?

Back in the château, the Marquis returned to his game, a disconcerting something rattling in the back of his mind. He couldn't stop thinking about all those tiny masked men he'd annihilated, and the trickles of black slime that flowed away from their broken little bodies.

4.

"Slime is the agony of water."

—SARTRE

Clones, or unwitting victims of some hideous fiction though they may have been, the masked men on their horses with their little (plastic!) swords each had his own really sad story to tell, just as the Marquis supposed. But it's hard to care for people you suspect might only be the surplus creation of the clever young people in CGI.

And if you're tempted to imagine that the masked figure in the house was more real than the others, or that he was in some way their leader, or the original template for the others, that may be true, perhaps it's very likely true, but I can offer no absolute assurances. You could ask him, but I doubt that he knows himself. If I'd known you were so curious, I could have waded out among his *muchachos* and their trampling steeds, but that would have been a fruitless task, perhaps even dangerous with all those freaky horses. Still, in all seriousness, a little disambiguation, *muchacho* from *muchacho*, would be welcome and helpful.

I know they'd be grateful if I told you just one of their stories, because all of them are heartbreaking. Now, when I think of them, bouncing around on those silly horses as if they were part of a possessed merry-go-round, I remember the fear and bewilderment in their eyes, sunk behind the tiny slits of their masks. Even now I do not know what sad and strange necessity it was that brought them to this desperate pass. Alien as they were, they were also somehow familiar, painfully familiar, like a childhood nightmare that you've never completely forgotten.

As for our friend in black, I think he was winging it. I cannot take seriously the idea that the message came from some Queen of Something living in the Hebrides, of all places. I mean, I don't even know where they are. (Islands, I take it.) Frankly, I think the masked man panicked when the men pressed him on the content of the letter and that he started making things up that he thought might impress them, or perhaps it was just that he thought they made him look good. Or important.

Contrary to the Marquis's claim that the letter was blank, there was indeed a message, a very simple thing, a request for a favor, and we'll come to that in time. But it's important to see that the little men on horseback also composed a message. Their message, as Islam teaches, was that there is no God but God. Their message, like God, was hidden in plain view. The milling horsemen in the courtyard, swarming over one another like black bugs, were the real bearers of the message; in fact they were the message. No wonder the poor lost souls looked so confused and disconsolate.

And what sort of message did they compose? No, seen from space they didn't form a shape, like something carved into a field of corn by aliens. Isn't it obvious? Their message was "contagion." Or contamination, the unbound cancer of an obscene and meaningless replication. The viral! For a virus is not a living thing, whether infectious agent or computer worm. It is a mere scrap of genetic coding no more complicated than on/off. It doesn't care if it destroys life and it doesn't care if it succeeds in surviving. It couldn't care less about competitive advantage. There is no such thing as a "successful" virus, a winner virus, it's all lost on them. Nor are viruses trying to be helpful in some way. The virus has something elemental to say and always has. If God ever spoke, it was as a virus. God said "Yes." Then he said "No." Then he said both at once and flickered like a neon sign with a loose connection. Out of that, believe it or not, came our perdurable world.

What has appalled these poor men in their Zorro outfits, and their cool hats, and their horsies that are God-knows-what (made out of biscuit dough as far as I know), and what has driven them to the tears of the unredeemed, is the creepy recognition that through them God is saying only, "No! By thunder, no! I have changed my mind. This was all a bad idea."

The men are less than a virus. They are oblivion.

You will see. You will see this. You will see.

5.

—after Rabelais

Once we understand that the message delivered by the masked man was "hidden in plain view," that it was in fact the messenger himself, the contagion of messengers and messages he brought, what followed begins to make sense.

I could begin anywhere, really, as you'll see, but for the sake of continuity I will begin near where we left off. Which is a shame because many people are more than glad for grand fissures in continuity, if for no other reason than that being wildly misled, or having their intelligence contravened, is preferable to the boredom of making sense and of having to convince the family dog that its dinner time is five, not three-thirty.

Anyway, the Marquis had a grandson, Jake. As a child, Jake would spend weekends with his grandpa, who'd make a very nice from-scratch pizza before retiring to the inner sanctum to play *Halo*. These pizzas that the Marquis lovingly made were really something. To see the smooth globes of dough sitting on the counter—a little dusting of flour on top like little round baby bottoms in talc—makes me sad to remember.

For they are surely gone. All gone.

Well, the kid could have grown up to live a straight, true, and happy life, but, man, things can get messed up. For Jake it was not so much the stuff that most kids have to go through these days, now that the maturing process and its rites of passage require the use of handguns. Like it or not, Glocks are the new normal for these kids. Like it or not, it's become part of growing up. That first court restraining order is now a milestone equal to a driver's license, high school diploma, college admission, and so on. Happily for Jake, the Marquis gave him a sort of happy, dopey reality apart from all that. As a consequence, he was as close to innocent as a young man could come in these withered days.

At a young age, Jake married and settled down in a modest split-level ranch house with his new wife, Fanni, let's call her. Jake learned to make pizza for her, just like his grandpa's, and they settled in for life . . . as it were. Here's the future *he* saw: he'd cook pizza and after dinner he and Fanni would play computer games, kissing now and then. On Fridays they'd have grandpa le Marquis over and play *Halo.* They'd drink root beer. What he neglected to figure into this delightful scenario was the fact that Fanni also had a notion or two about what married life ought to be like. Unfortunately for Jake, she was of the opinion that her life with her husband ought to be different in important ways from her husband's life with his grandpa. In particular, the eating of pizzas and the playing of computer games was boring to the point of wishing that her high school biology teacher would come by and "pith" her with a straight pin in the frontal lobe, just as he'd done with frogs. After a month or so of Jake's idea of happiness, buyer's remorse was the primary fact of her life.

Jake was a simple person. Fanni was not a simple person. She did not have Jake's stable, happy background sharing time with a grandparent in blissful side-by-side interface with the good old Xbox. What Fanni had was a single mother who lived on the left side of a brick duplex in the spiritually destitute region just south of Chicago. Their house was one of those structures that census workers look at and say, "Does this count?" Her mother supported their little family through frequent "presents" from various "close family friends" in the form of cocaine or cash equivalents. What these friends got in return is irrelevant or almost. In spite of all that, Fanni grew up a smart kid capable of wandering away from the daily horror show at the old duplex. She thrived at school, went to college, met the son of a Marquis (!) and, without giving it a lot of thought, married.

In the sad thereafter, their marriage counselor suggested to her that she should have known what Jake was like; she'd been to his house before they married, hadn't she? And she said, "Yes, I knew what he was like, but I thought he was kidding." Then she added, "And he did kiss me once under the grain elevator, and so I asked him with my eyes to ask me, and when he did I thought, 'Well, as well him as another.'"

Jake was sitting right there, holding her hand as she said these hurtful things. The therapist's response was to put his head in his hands (the closest he could come to neutral affect in the moment). The counselor, at least, knew that it was too late and Fanni had already gone to blazes. On the other hand, he could now also confirm that Jake's form of innocence was, just as Fanni claimed, morally exhausting. He could see how it could drive a person to unpleasant extremes.

As for Jake, he didn't yet quite know what to make of it all. But when he saw the counselor bury his head in his hands he had to wonder, "Is that how I should be responding to what she's saying?" He looked at her sitting by his side. She was smiling pleasantly.

There was something damaged in Fanni, something broken. She was, in a sense, not "there," not present. For instance, she could not seem to tell the difference between the good things that she did and the bad things. Make breakfast? Hit their barky Yorkie with a shovel? Essentially the same for her. But when Jake showed how they were not the same, she would get confused and start crying. "How can you be so sure about everything?" she'd ask, and then she'd go after the dog with a hoe because it had stuck its cold snout inside her summer shorts and smelled her fur. (She kept garden implements in the kitchen for such moments.)

She was also someone with the interesting and organic conviction that if the world spread out from her, it was her job to take it all back in. Perhaps it was some sort of bizarre maternal instinct gone wrong, but she had faith in the thought that everything should go back to her empty inside.

And then there was the shopping. She shopped with tenacity, knowing that it was her responsibility to buy it all, to take it all inside. She was the Imelda Marcos of any- and everything. She didn't shop *in* Big Box stores, she shopped *for* Big Box stores. She created shopping lists like the card catalogue at the Library of Alexandria.

When she wasn't shopping, she was eating. Unfortunately, this duty, this "moral imperative to internalize the world," had horrible consequences in restaurants. She did not understand the purpose of a menu. The idea that she should choose only one thing from each section—one salad, one entrée, etc.—simply made no sense to her. The idea that there were sections didn't make sense to her. Appetizer. Entrée. What? Explain as Jake surely did, it was all beyond her. She thought Jake was yammering metaphysics when all he might be saying was, "Darling, you don't start with the chocolate mousse. It's not an appetizer." There were some meals that took the form of quest legends. It was as if she believed that there was some food, some perfect food, that would make her world right if only she could find it. In spite of all his goodness and his love for her, Jake lacked the will to enforce what he called, for her benefit, "food reality."

When he said things like that, in what she took to be a know-ing and superior way, she would say, "There is nothing so dull as innocence."

Touché!

Once during the Christmas season Jake and Fanni were eat-ing at the legendary Stockyard Trough down in Decatur. She started in her pell-mell way with a dilled *Blanquette de Veau*. The chef had prepared six portions for the evening and she ate them all. She followed that with dozens of pizza hot-pockets off the children's menu. (Yes, some of the little darlings cried when they were told that there were no more pizza hot-pockets, but she insisted that some people would have to sacrifice for the greater good, and she volunteered the children.)

The headwaiter scrambled with a sponge to erase the fea-tured dishes as they fell from the little chalkboard out front, inexorably, one after another. At neighboring tables, the wait-ers sensed the drift of things and started encouraging guests to order quickly while there was still something more than bread and butter to eat.

"What!!??" one obese old-timer complained, a Cargill seed cap cockeyed on his head, bloody stains from rib-eyes past on his overalls. "No beef? None at all? Not even an old piece of flank? Not even a burger? How is that possible? This is the Stockyard Trough, isn't it? Do you know what a stockyard is? What's that you say? Her? That little girl over there with the Marquis's boy? Are you saying she's eaten the entire cow? I'll be damned!"

Having decimated the main courses, she retreated to the soups and polished off one pot each of borscht, split pea, and *soup du jour*, potato/leek. ("André! Scratch the soups!") At this point she observed that her napkin was soiled and asked for another. Pitiless, she ate the herbed caviar roulade, the crepes with caviar filling, potatoes with caviar, caviar éclairs, oysters and caviar, and—a *coup de main, de resistance, de théâtre, d'état, de grâce,* and *de foudre*—a cobbler with knuckle truffles (the low, obsequious sort common to the Aberdeens), creamed clotters, and crushed sweet-rind. (If you're looking for the recipe, it's in Mark Bittman's *Cobblers and Gobblers: Cooking with Cottage Clusters and Custard Clotters.*)

And why did she eat these things? She ate these things because that's just the kind of gal she was.

6.

"But you know, no matter where we are
We're always touching by underground wires."

—OF MONTREAL

But what brought Fanni and Jake and their marriage to a dangerous point was sex. At first, living in the country, consumed with the imperatives of shopping and eating, she hardly knew that sex existed. But one day she discovered (while strolling through the Web seeking to find things that she could buy all of) that she could perhaps also consume other human beings. Seriously, she sat upright, stared straight ahead, and had a little epiphany. Consuming people! Of course. Why had she not thought of this before?

So she joined a Web group called "Sex Gorging with Friends." There were people out there, aware of the needs of the gorgers, who essentially offered themselves, on the site, for ready consumption. Basically, they said, as you might expect, "Eat me," but they also said more complicated things like "I'm lonely" or "Let's party" or "Want to date?"

There's something weirdly sweet about these little expressions one finds on porn sites. It's as if they were the childish nothings that are written on those tiny, heart-shaped Valentine's Day candies that kids pass out at school. "Kiss me!" "Bite me!" "Fist me!" "Ass Maul™ me." It was then that she had a vision, an apotheosis, if you will, that she must take everything, all the boys, as well as the girls, inside. Like some louche Rabelaisian conceit, she would crouch beneath the sex tree, heavy with fruit, spread wide her thighs, and shake them all down into her cavernous interior.

Soon Fanni had the triple burden of bringing home U-Hauls loaded with the day's purchases, eating all of the chocolate decadence cookies in the world, all the spit-roasted chickens at every convenience store, and balling as many boys and girls as possible in motels all across central Illinois. A carnival it was, both comical and obscene.

When Jake complained to his grandfather about his wife, the Marquis replied wisely, "She is the wife of the grandson of the Marquis de N—. Her life *should* be given over to the frantic spending of extravagant wealth, to no purpose at all, sure only that she lives on the labor of others. She must sacrifice and empty all being, but not by swallowing it, for God's sake. She is being too literal. It must be entirely *wasted* to be worthy of our lineage. Thrown out on the ground, if you will. Over time, even the slaves come to understand the wisdom of this arrangement. For what we throw on the ground becomes their livelihood. I don't call that complicated.

"You could be better at this yourself. Honestly, I think there's something of the mystic mendicant in you. What do you do with the money I throw at you? Give it to that woman so that she can pursue mere *things*? The point is the infinite emptying out of the thing-in-itself in the spectacle of barren consumption.

Is that so hard to understand? No one should actually want the crappy shit! Let alone want to take it inside them! We are not a digestive system! We are aristocrats! The landed gentry! Where did you find this ragamuffin child, in some Aurora condo?"

"Actually, yes, that's where she grew up, as I told you."

"Oh, I knew I'd gotten the idea from somewhere. I assumed that you had the good sense to be lying about it."

There was not even a moment's solace for him when the Marquis suggested that, if all else failed, she might be stoned at the city periphery, under the freeway overpass near the new Home Depot. That's where that sort of thing usually took place. After all, unlike spending money, ruthless sexual roistering was *exclusively* the prerogative of the oligarch *boys*, as far as the Marquis was concerned, and he knew his stuff regarding the ancient protocols. The girls, and especially the wives, he said, could just "sit on their tuffets." But after a moment's fantastic conjuring of this stoning, Jake remembered that his grandfather was from an older and very conservative generation. Attractive as it was, stoning was probably out of the question in the world as presently construed.

Contrary to what Jake may have thought, Fanni got nothing out of all this—not prestige, not wealth, not the love of her community—and she certainly did not get anything like what we would understand as pleasure. She did it all out of a sense of duty. She did it because she was obedient. She followed the instructions delivered by the inner voice of the world. In fact, she was so pure that she put to shame the world itself. Seen in the right light, she was beatific. She fulfilled prophecy. In the sad end, when Jake asked her to explain herself, she said, severely, "I am." Like those of the Sphinx, her victims festooned the rocks below while she gazed innocently at the horizon.

7.

*"It is madness to suppose one owes something to one's mother . . .
She casts us into a world beset with dangers, and once in it, 'tis
for us to manage as best we can."*

—THE MARQUIS DE SADE

I don't want to make it seem as if the sexual troubles experienced by Jake and Fanni were in any way out of the ordinary.
They were simply part—a very vivid part, agreed—of the Way
of the World, as the following news item attests.

THE CHILDREN MUST LEAVE

(AP) In a legal decision that will be debated and reinterpreted
for decades, the Supreme Court ruled on the constitutionality
of several recent state and municipal laws seeking to use civil
confinement against potential sex criminals, especially potential pedophiles but also rapists, sexual cannibals, and those who
perform "unnatural acts with the beasts of the field" (Arkan-
sas, Oklahoma, and Texas). What is extraordinary is that the
Court let stand several federal appeals court decisions affirm-
ing the constitutionality of laws in Vermont, Oregon, and other
states allowing mass preventive detention of people who only
might commit sex crimes against children. Some of the people
who brought suit are presently in detention even though they
have not committed a crime. Of course, it is impossible in most
cases to know their true intentions, and so they have been called
"malefactors in sexual thought crimes against children."

Most of those presently in detention are there solely on the
testimony of friends and relatives, although there is a surpris-
ingly large number who have self-identified as sex criminals *in*

potentia and turned themselves in, many with elaborate written accounts, duly notarized, of the pedophilic acts they haven't committed.

Asked to explain the thinking behind Oregon's version of this law, the state attorney general, Lisa Mulhern, said, "Our law requires little explanation. These are our *children* we are talking about. They deserve our protection."

Critics of the laws claim that they violate the equal protection clause of the Fourteenth Amendment since the laws identify particular classes of people vulnerable to the laws, especially priests (reasonably), but also wicked uncles, and "old men who live alone" (West Virginia), as well as novel categories like "sexual cannibals." Critics also complain of the vagueness of the laws since uncles are also, in other connections, fathers and husbands and brothers. Finally, critics worry that the laws will be convenient vehicles for retribution for other insults or imagined injuries that may be entirely the invention of the accuser.

In an eleventh-hour amicus briefing, the ACLU—an organization composed almost entirely of adults, the Court noted—argued that it was the children who should be confined. Again, the Court did not find this persuasive.

Although analysis of this historic decision has just begun, legal scholars seem to agree that in theory *everyone* is now subject to civil confinement as a potential child sex predator, rapist, or sexual cannibal. When Ms. Greta Kosar, a spokesperson for the Court, was asked if this meant that everyone should now consider him- and herself to be in theoretical civil confinement, she smiled and commented, "That is a plausible outcome of the Court's logic, yes."

"Does that include members of the Court itself?"

"I can only say that the Court does not mean to needlessly alarm the public. These laws will not be enforced capriciously but only where appropriate and on a case-by-case basis. The Court has had this assurance from the states, and we trust them to be responsible."

Finally, in Vermont, the tiny Roman Catholic hamlet of Further Enrichment concluded that the only way to be certain to avoid the implications of the Court's rulings was to drive the town's residents beneath the age of sixteen to the county line and warn them not to return until they are of age. While a few parents complained about this preemptive action, most others seemed relieved. One neighbor commented, "It was a necessary thing to do. You can't live with that sort of uncertainty. They were a provocation with lunchboxes. For a close-knit community like ours, that's just not acceptable. Nevertheless, they are our kids and we wish them all the best." The village priest observed that the expulsion was appropriate under the Church's "proximity to sin" doctrine. (A papal encyclical titled "At Arm's Length" will be posted to the Vatican's website on Thursday.)

At the time of this report, none of the children of Further Enrichment have retained legal representation. Given today's Supreme Court decision, it seems unlikely that many—if any— lawyers will want to take on the professional and personal risks.

One Burlington public defender commented, "It's really a puzzle to me how these kids could ever obtain legal representation. After all, wouldn't lawyer-client confidentiality, with its faintly scabrous suggestion of private meetings behind closed doors, make the attorney vulnerable to the new confinement laws? In fact, since the laws specify *preventive* confinement, it would be prudent of state bar associations if they announced publicly that none of their members will represent anyone sixteen and younger in the current legal climate. Even that is no guarantee, given the expansiveness of the ruling."

Of the town's affected children, only three-year-old Tommy

Rogers of rural Further Enrichment was willing to take questions from reporters. When asked what he thought of the Court's decision, he replied boldly, "What are why here? Ha! Here come *meeee!*"

Residents last reported seeing Tommy, his hand held by his older sister Tammy Rogers, age 8, walking south on State Highway 10 toward the Massachusetts border where there was rumored to be an aid station set up by the Department of Homeland Security.

8.

Faust: "This damned Here!"

—GOETHE

Fanni grew up in a brick apartment on a cracked concrete slab in suburban Chicago (it was, in fact, Aurora). There was a Casey's and a Dollar Store down the block. Her mother's only possession, other than her clothes, was a 1967 Dodge Dart with bald tires and a leaky radiator. Fanni has a photograph of her mother sitting in the driver's seat of the Dodge, its window down, her arm cocked on the ledge as if she were a person in control. In control of the vehicle, in control of her life. She is smiling.

Unfortunately, it is not true that she was in control of anything. To show this, let us take this photo, open it up, and spread its contents out on a table in order to get a better understanding of just what is *in* this photograph. Once it is opened up in this detailed way, we notice that her blouse is not fresh. We notice that she appears to have gum disease. In the pupils of her eyes, one can clearly see that the person she is smiling at is her drug dealer. (His elongated convex image is also present in the rear passenger's window.) We could further deduce that she is "going out" and leaving her daughter with the drug dealer, who will be asked to serve as babysitter. (His name was Alphonse and he was actually very nice to the daughter when he was conscious. He protected her from the next-door neighbor, about whom more in a moment.) The only thing that is really clear is that she is entirely lacking in self-knowledge while being vain and self-absorbed, a very taxing combination of traits.

And yet if you saw her today you would swear she is pretty, and indeed she is!

Her father is a high school teacher in Naperville. He teaches science. He filed for divorce when Mom took Ecstasy and brought home a "friend from the motorcycle club" named Filthy. Filthy was a very civic-minded man and helped administer the club's (invitation only) "Cocaine is Commerce" convention and charity fundraiser. The club thought this convention was funny, but local addicts enjoyed the free samples whether the convention was a joke or not. For her father, there did not seem to be a question of who should stay and who should go, so he left. As for Filthy, they finally got rid of him when Alphonse declared that he was a bad influence on Fanni, but the truth is that he was only willing to leave when he was given a cigar box full of Alphonse's best cannabis.

Nothing about teaching high school biology prepared Fanni's father for this sort of behavior in a wife. When he left, he looked as if he were a small furry mammal kept in a shoebox on which a brick has been dropped. The court awarded custody to Mom, and Dad got visitation rights that seemed to have something to do with leap years. As far as the court was concerned, a very prudent principle had been maintained: a young child needs its mother.

It was a fine piece of work all the way around. And I haven't even come to what lived next door in the dismal little duplex in which she was now doomed to grow up. Her neighbor, a person that she shared a wall with, a very thin wall, was a man in jeans with a crotch so filthy that it looked as if it had been used to strain clotted cream.

"Hi, honey," he would say to her, "Watcha got there? A dolly?"

This is where Alphonse would say, "*Chingate, cabrón*. No to bother her, *pendejo*." Sometimes he took out a knife to make his point more vivid, but, as I mentioned, at other times he was "away."

This was the karmic condition into which she was born, like it or not. It all came to maturity twenty years down the road when Fanni married Jake and invited him to watch as a craigslist "handyman" plowed her hindwise with a virile member whose permanent readiness for such chores defies the studious attention of the contemplative mind.

But if you think that I am suggesting that Fanni was a monster, a slut, fallen, cruel, deranged, or even just a little carried away, that is a mistake. For, in a sense, Fanni was just one of the many. Hurtful as she was for young Jake, she was just doing what everybody was suddenly doing as if they too were, like the little men on horses, just copies of something. She was just an expression of something beyond herself. God? Fate? Genes? Neurons? Who knows? What is important is not to blame her for the usual things, her tragic flaws or her sins, because she lacked nothing, she was not acquisitive, she was not a "shopper," she was not a gourmand, and she was not a sexual predator. She just was what many were. I wouldn't want to call it a *belle époque*, but it was an epoch. She was simply of her moment. I would go so far as to say that if there was someone having trouble fitting in, it was innocent Jake. Many of Fanni's new friends even commented that he wasn't a "people person."

I believe, to put it metaphysically, and that's really the way it should be put, that Fanni was part of a spiritual warp in space that had caused the cosmic monkey soul to go digitally viral. (But who can blame her for that? No one intends with malice aforethought to be the catalyst for a new version of cosmic monkey soul. Agreed?) Almost everyone in the community, but all the women for sure, found themselves caught in a strange compulsion, a wretchedness, in which they were not at all unlike the black-clad messengers on horseback with whom we began this tale. No one "wanted" to do any of this. They had no idea what they were doing or why they were doing it. They found themselves carried before a gale, as if a strong hand were pressing at the smalls of their backs. They drifted as if they were caught in the solar winds that move about in the empty regions of space, ionized bits purling in warm currents made by coronal emissions.

What troubling nights those were for us! At five a.m. the sidewalks would be crowded with townsfolk taking the walk of shame back to whatever was left of their families. The men's underwear would look as if someone had dumped a cup of yoghurt in them. The women would stare vacantly, stricken smiles on their faces, futilely holding their now buttonless blouses together with trembling hands.

As for the matrix of computers that made this lubricious commonality possible, it was as if it had a virus that was more like a venereal disease than something requiring a security patch. Something had contaminated the inner mind of the digital realm, creating a sort of alphanumeric fever-dream where a deviant /PCI0@0/SATA@A/PRT0@ in the Universal Device Tree had been uploaded into all of these poor folk, complete with peculiar tendencies. Yes, again, contagion! And yet, for those involved, there was nothing artificial or consumer-electronic about their experiences. For them it all felt more like the revelation of an ancient identity, something to be found at the apexes of pyramids while a priestly caste looks on. This identity had long eluded them, but now it was very near and very clear and very, very dear.

"So this is what I am," they said, and smiled.

And so, with cheerful resignation, they got on with it.

9.

"What is most holy in me is delivered up to mockery."
—JOHANN FICHTE

Her name was Felicité. You don't know her, but you know of her. She was that woman of great power and wealth alluded to by the Masked Messenger. It was she who sent him on his errand.

To her less-than-familiars, she was the forbidding Queen of Spells. Her ancient and noble clan had long ago established their demesne on the tiny Isle of Islay in the Outer Hebrides. They fell in love with Islay, a place of fairies, magic, and mystery. They soon learned the dark arts of the island, and over the generations these occult skills were enlarged, perfected, and at last given to this precocious young girl. A great dark power was hers, but she never used it for dark purposes. For she was not interested in the wizardry of skulduggery and political machinations; rather, she was a sort of wizard poet. Like Manfred, she could summon any spirit she liked, but she could also create beneficial spirits and name them.

Her wisdom, like the Buddha's, was "do no harm," and she didn't. Well, not on purpose, she didn't. But, as you will have observed yourself, once you start doing things, other things follow, unanticipated things, and these are frequently such as can be accurately described as harmful or even catastrophic. Things accumulate and stumble drunkenly, by which point if there hasn't been some sort of bloody muck-up, it's a miracle, a real bewilderment. Call me gloomy, the Queen always did, but that's how the world looks to me. "The best procedure is to sit on your hands, hold your breath, and hope for the best," I'd say to her. She'd just stare at me and shake her lovely head sadly and say, "You disappoint me!"

"Oh, bright eyes!" I'd retort.

At any rate, it was she created the somber messenger and sent him on his baffled way to N— and the Marquis. In saying that she, the Queen of Spells, had made this messenger, I do not mean to say that he was for her a mere piece of wizard gadgetry, some hollow husk into which she had sighed her sweet but indifferent breath. She didn't make many of the perplexed golems, but when she did she always did so reverently. She cared about her guys, is the way I'd put it. She even went to the trouble of giving them names (in this case "Percy"), even though they rarely remembered them. She sent them on their missions with some anxiety, knowing that what she asked of them might be dangerous, and knowing just how poorly prepared they were to deal with the busy, self-seeking, and malign world of humans.

On the subject of these malign humans: I have learned that when a certain kind of human would discover that the Queen's creations were not-quite-human, something seemed to click in

them, click in a wrong sort of way, click as in: "What I'm hearing here, Mrs. Islay, is that I can do just about anything to this
puppet without any moral considerations. Right? Am I missing
something? If I'm understanding this . . . what would you call
him? This moist duffel bag [!?] is more like an inflatable sex doll
than he is like us humans. (Well, maybe not more like a sex
doll than Marcia over there, but still, you know what I mean. By
the way, can someone see if she's still breathing?) So yessss, by
all means, you may leave him here. We'll take good care of him.
I may even tap a keg of Old Style and invite some friends over to
celebrate his presence among us. Oh, one last thought, does this
thing have a memory? I mean, could it like *testify*?"

Anyway, in order to make her more recent creations, like
Percy, feel a little safer in their work, keep them a little further
from the predations of the wrong sort of human, she also created a small army of companions for support. They were too
tiny to offer physical protection, unfortunately, but they could
provide moral witness. For some reason, their little staring eyes
did dampen the enthusiasm of the moderately horrible humans.
(The utterly horrible didn't care if they watched or not. They
even seemed to like an audience.) Unlike Percy, once these tiny
companions had served their modest purpose, the chaps were
usually vacuumed up, recycled, or otherwise rendered as live-
stock feed or nutritional supplements.

But this was all several months ago, now. She had said to
Percy, "Deliver this message to the Marquis of N— in Illinois,
USA. If all goes well, he will give us a royal brevet allowing
ourselves special privileges." It should have taken no more than
a week, even if processing the little companions had delayed
things at customs.

And in this case there was quite a delay. To the customs agents
and airport security, Percy's companions looked like a bunch

of wind-up toys set loose—running into one another, falling down—and Percy had his hands full as they staggered around the room. The federal marshals screamed at them to drop or step back or raise or spread, they couldn't seem to agree on what they wanted, nothing of which the little darlings understood, bless them. They were cheap things and tottered stiffly when not on their horsies, and, from a security perspective, why weren't they suicide bombers, maybe? With little tiny explosive vests capable, say, of blowing up a Kleenex box. I'd say the U.S. agents were entirely in the right when they shot a few of them, just to test their mettle. Unfortunately, as with the trigger-happy Marquis just a few days in the future, the cops seemed to get carried away, and soon there was a regular police riot, with bullets flying around errantly as if Fearless Fosdick were doing the shooting. In the final body count, a regular variety pack of foreign nationals of the "little brown" sort were killed along with the leprechauns on horseback. Of course, being in any sense threatening was often worse than mere death in those days of extraordinary rendition, ghost detainees, black sites, torture by proxy, and extrajudicial detainment. In fact, once the little fellas were given entrance to the country, there was a worrisome little fella remainder, those who were KIA or arrested. The Masked Messenger tried to pursue the issue, knowing how unhappy Felicité would be if she started getting postcards from Guantanamo, but the Feds took a hose and squeegee to what was left of the kills, and Percy and his remaining companions were escorted out of the terminal and into waiting vans with blackened windows.

Well, anyway, that was their hard luck, the little fellas, and after all they weren't real, even if they were prone to tears, and so I won't waste any more of your time on them. It's not as if the mayhem got on CNN or anything, although it might have minus the White House news blackout. But I do hate to think of the unaccounted leprechauns in an open cage somewhere south, sweltering behind their little masks, squatting in their own shit on a concrete floor, little black bags over their heads, sobbing while Chihuahuas sniffed at their crotches, while overhead indifferent palm trees waved, as if they saw an old friend at the other end of the beach.

But then, for reasons not even she could explain, she forgot about Percy. Distracted? Was he like a pan of milk she'd been heating absentmindedly until with a start she smelled it overflowing into the flames and burning? Whatever the case, eventually his absence worried her. The little men didn't concern her. If they'd returned, she would just have melted them down in the big pot out back until they were once again the flabby cack that they'd come from. But she had plans for Percy.

In her mind, Percy had potential. He was what she called a "good one." She honestly thought he would do well at one of those technical institutes that the Americans were so pleased with. He'd have to apply himself because, hard as she tried, she could never quite make her creatures anything like what you'd call bright. Still, she could just see him in a little cubicle, his happy workspace, his computer before him, smiling in a way that was both happy and idiotic. How proud she'd be! The only thing she worried about was his tendency to be a little melodramatic. Even though he was not really alive as such, in any strict sense of alive, he had this strange habit of claiming that his life was in danger. This sometimes made things difficult for him in the midst of the little chores he was given. Stranger yet, when he got that way, there was just no reasoning with him. Once he got started, it was all atrocities (that was a favorite) and bloodthirsty fiends pursuing him, threatening to cut his throat. It was disturbing to a lot of the people he met. She probably should have given him a little card to hand out explaining his peculiar behavior, as if he were just someone with a theatrical case of Tourette's.

Eventually, even though she hated to travel, she decided that she had to go after him herself. You are probably wondering why she didn't just send another golem out after him, but she'd tried that in the past and it didn't work. After a day or two, the searching golem would return and say, "Let me get this straight. Someone is looking for me, right?" "No! You are doing the seeking!" And off he'd go only to return a few days later, saying, "Okay, could you go over that again?"

No, that would not do, especially for a creature as important to her as Percy. So she said, "While the nigh thatch smokes in the sun-thaw, and the eave-drops fall in the trances, let my secret ministry be done with radial arm saws!" And so saying she traced his route to distant N— determined to find him, set him up in an apartment, and enroll him at Corn Belt Community College. This was all she really wanted from the Marquis and his brevet: a little help signing him up for some vocational courses that would allow him to be not merely a wizard's golem but a suitably employed data drone.

How Percy or the Marquis could have got such a simple purpose messed up was beyond her. But even as fond as she was of the "instant peasants" (her term) that she created, she knew that they almost never did anything entirely right. There was always a sort of messy surplus, a gory shirttail hanging out the back and leaving a trail of blood behind.

10.

"There are ancient and modern poems that breathe the divine spirit of irony throughout . . . there is in them a truly transcendental buffoonery."

—FRIEDRICH SCHLEGEL

Anxious about the approaching meeting with the Queen of Spells, the Marquis asked Rory if there had been any omens recently in the form of prodigies that might provide a sense of what to expect. Rory's face drained of color, and he stared at his interlocutor, hanging fire.

"What in the world is the matter? You're hanging fire," said the Marquis.

"I'm afraid to say, sir."

"For God's sake, why?"

"There have been such prodigies, sir, and many of them."

Now it was the Marquis's turn to drain of color.

"Well, you'd better tell me then."

"Yes, sir. First, sir, remember that these were told me by simple and superstitious people."

"Oh, you mean over in Peoria. Those people barely know to live in houses."

"There and elsewhere, sir."

"All right, then, get on with it."

Rory took out a piece of paper on which he'd scribbled notes.

"First, it was reported in Leroy that a vine shoot burst into flame. It rained chalk in Downs, and blood in Funk's Grove. In Springfield a statue of Abraham Lincoln moved forward of its own volition. Finally, a cow in Towanda talked."

"Good Lord, what did it say?"

"It said, 'I am one who eats her breakfast watching morning glories.'"

"Obviously!"

"I think the point is that it talked at all."

"Understood, but all the same, if it's going to go to the trouble of talking, it ought to say something worth hearing. Not just ungulate banalities."

"As you like, sir. If I may, ungulate is a very fine word. I thank you for it. I shall share it with my wife this evening."

"Rory, you've been working for me for many years and I did not know you had a wife. I thought you were of another persuasion."

"Sir?"

Awkward pause.

"The jocose persuasion, of course."

"Ah, jocose. I thought you might be suggesting that I was a faggot."

"Rory!"

"Shall I proceed, sir?"

"Go ahead, but be careful. We don't want to create an uncomfortable work environment for the cleaning bitch. The feds are watching because Tuesday the Laotians in security beat some spics, and the next day the greasers in security beat some gooks. I don't mind that, but once the courts get involved . . . the paperwork!"

"Sir, you quite amaze me."

The Marquis nodded humbly.

"It's the aura of nobility."

"Quite so. Then in Lexington there was a great commotion because a child in the womb shouted, 'Hurrah!'"

"My God! A fetus, you say? What was he hurrahing?"

"I cannot say, sir. A fetus shouting anything was sufficient, I believe, to catch their simple attention."

"True enough. But I wonder how they heard it. I mean, just how loud could a little fetus, a mere tangle of unresolved coding, be?"

"That's what I said, sir, but there were many that claimed to hear it quite clearly. They said that the youngster was celebrating General Beauregard's victory at First Manassas."

"Little late for that, isn't it?"

"The South, it is said, will rise again."

"So I've heard. Well, is there more?"

"Oh yes, sir, there's always more. In Chenoa, a woman changed her sex."

"To what?"

"She is now a dog being rained on."

"Does she call that a sex?"

"I asked her that and she said, 'I am whitened bones in a field.'"

"That is not a prodigy. She must be one of the homeless lunatics that I'm supposed to do something about, God knows what."

"In Pontiac an altar appeared in the sky with men in white robes around it."

"That's better. Pontiac has always been a reliable place. A very sober lot, the Pontiac."

"In Peru, graves yawned and yielded up their dead."

"Wow!"

"And in Eureka, fierce, fiery warriors fought in the clouds, and drizzled blood on the town. The noise of battle was hurled this way then that, in the air, and horses neighed while ghosts shrieked and squealed in the streets."

"That's terrific! Those are what I call omens!"

"There's more. In Dwight, a swarm of bees was mistaken for an invasion of armed men."

"Oh, come on. Now you've ruined everything. A swarm of bees? That's ridiculous."

"Not for the townspeople who slaughtered their own wives and children, despairing that they would fall into the hands of the bee-like barbarians."

"Are you making this stuff up?"

"Sir, you asked for prodigies."

"Yes, but real prodigies like armies fighting in the clouds."

"Please not to blame the messenger, my liege."

"All right. At long last, is that all?"

"Yes, sir, except that in Streater the soothsayers required propitiatory rights and full-grown victims were sacrificed."

"Full-grown what? Not people, surely."

"Yes. The priests said it was done because they were too many."

"Too many people?"

"'Too many people in Streator' is the way he put it."

"That's awful, but just like those priests. Between you and me, I see their point. I mean about Streator."

"You may be consoled to know that the sacrifices were followed by a period of prayer led by the Mayor."

"Mayor Cachesex? That drunk?"

"Sir, it is said that a flower dies even though we love it, and a weed grows even though we do not love it."

"Oh, this is hopeless."

"Did you know that in Joliet a man of livid hue on the city planner's staff found that his late model, low mileage, foreign import (a Kia, to be exact) had been replaced by a one-horse chaise once known as a cabriolet? And all while he ate his supper."

"Won't you please shut up!?"

"I won't claim that as a prodigy, but I do think it bears look-ing into."

"Well, I won't look into it, if it's all the same to you. None-theless, this little talk has calmed me, perhaps because you are so stupid that if worse comes to worst I'll be happy to die just so I won't have to listen to you anymore."

"Sir!"

"Ah, Rory, the valiant only taste of death but once."

"Indeed that's so, sir!"

11.

"We are shackled to this bomb we call the body."

—PLATO

Once at the Marquis's château, it was much easier for the Queen to gain entrance than it had been for the hyperbolic Percy. It helped that she arrived at an appointed time and in the middle of the afternoon. Rory answered the door. There were no lies about the wrong house or the wrong marquis. She was admitted with a deep and respectful bow.

"Right this way. The Marquis is expecting you."

Actually, dreading would have been a better word.

The Marquis had many reasons to dread a conversation with Felicité, none of them having to do with omens. His anxieties were particular and substantial. He dreaded her visit because he resented her and would have a hard time not showing that fact. He resented her because she was a queen and somehow he was just a marquis. In his envious mind that made his title sound too much like he was a mere small-time founder of one of those newfangled startup firms that don't actually seem to make or sell anything in particular. Companies with names like Kinetic Dispositions, Ltd. If you were to ask this founder just what his company did, he'd say something like, "We articulate systemic dispositions when underlying complexities are obscure. You've probably seen our work in relation to triadic analyses of abandoned market vistas." Later, back in his gaudy corner office, the founder smirks and plays *Angry Birds* on his telephone, just as our do-nothing Marquis whacks *Halo* aliens. The difference, of course, is that Kinetic Dispositions will shortly offer an IPO and its founder will retire a billionaire, while the Marquis will be stuck in his decaying château with no one to talk to but Rory.

Although he disliked this feeling, this diminution, this confusion about his own legitimate rank, it was in truth the underlying reality of all historic nobilities: they have power, they have wealth, but they have no idea how to explain why that's so, how it happened, or what good, exactly, they do, if they do anything at all beyond protect their own prerogatives behind a miserable façade of lying abstractions. The only difference between the *ancienne regime* and the modern financier, our corporate plutocrat, is that the old nobility played whist. That was the subconscious confusion for our Marquis: at some dim level of his mind he knew that he should be playing card games, looking out over a meticulously geometrical garden, snorting snuff, and signing off on decapitations. Instead, he was living in total abstraction, an almost metaphysical isolation amidst stands of corn or their stubble, and addicted to killing digital ghosts while smoking hashish. The world had gone wrong. Here, the peasants owned all the land, and the nobility had a front lawn. How much more at peace with the world he would be if he had a guillotine.

In relation to the Queen, his resentment was even heavier on his heart. Why did she get to be a queen? Why did she live on a romantic island of sages and sorcerers changing the course of history and influencing weather systems while he was in some midwestern gulag wondering what exactly the farmers did all day? He liked being *The Marquis*, and he liked lording it over the homeless and the droids in their lackey carrels over at Corporate South, about as alive as eggs in a carton. But when he was visited by a noble of superior rank, he knew he was just another rube. He knew that after the Queen's visit he'd have to find his therapist's cellphone number, and set up useless counseling sessions that would stretch into infinity, and talk about how his daddy was a real marquis, the real deal, but that he'd always felt so very small and weak, only a little marquis. All that pathetic talking, and revealing, and making-humble with someone whose only claim to credibility was an MA gained after twelve years of night school at North Southeastern Illinois State Extension Campus for Non-Traditional Students in Joliet, where classes were held in unused meeting rooms at the federal penitentiary. All this when what he wanted was so simple: to feel omnipotent. To own everything. To be ubiquitous. And fucking queens from mystical lands made that difficult.

Worse yet, there was the power issue, the *puissance* issue. The Queen, he well knew, could actually do stuff. She could put the hammer down. If she wanted shock and awe, she had it. She didn't just brag to the peasants about it with no more follow-through than what an adolescent acquires from his Game Boy. All he had was a ridiculous "security force" mostly composed of minimum-wage day laborers, a mixture of Haitians, Nicaraguans, Sudanese, and, since Iceland had been put into receivership by the World Bank (its people ejected, put out in the North Atlantic in great flotillas of human flotsam) a whole lot of super-clean blond people who didn't like sitting next to or being touched by the sullied Haitians. Which would have been great, the Icelanders were so pleasant to look at, a real feather in a marquis's hat, except that they were so depressed and drank so many vodka slushies and just sort of spent their days running their tongues along the soiled rill of the world, that in the end he preferred the Haitians, especially when they spent their lunch hour sitting on the curb running their hands over their weathered faces and rheumy eyes. They were colorful and exotic, and they made more firm the fact that there *was* still a difference between a nobleman and his peasants.

Anyway, this security force was adequate for the purposes of driving poor people off the Marquis's front lawn—as when the Occupy the Marquis people were around—but other than that they were a joke. A violent joke, but a joke. These day-labor goon squads really got off on violent repression, never mind that if they didn't get the "c'mon" sign to get in the pickup truck the next morning, they'd be among the lumpen mass themselves, driven around with cattle prods, billy clubs, and rubber bullets by the very people they themselves had brutalized the day before.

All of this—what? security simulacrum?—made the Marquis disconsolate. He couldn't even afford to buy Tasers for his agents. But what he most wanted was not slaughter in *Halo,* not Haitians beating people on the front lawn, he wanted a *secret* police. How important and generally *puissant* that would make him feel. He fantasized about the conversations he would have with his Midwestern Metternich.

The Marquis might say, "Oh, so you take the rascal away in the middle of the night, his wife and children grasping at his feet, and you put him in secret confinement. Then in the morning when the abandoned wife and children complain to the non-secret police, they can claim that they know nothing about it. They'll say that he must have been up to something dangerous and now his family must suffer for his folly. They'll say that he was probably kidnapped by a drug gang. This is very clever, isn't it? And then you do whatever you like. Surely torture is involved? Yes, why not indeed! Is it possible that you reserve a special day each month for visitors? I don't mean to be imprudent about this, but does it ever happen that, say, an important person could pop over just to see how it's done, the torturing? Not to interfere, but just to satisfy his noble curiosity? Yes? Lovely. What time do these torture sessions ordinarily begin? Not too late, I hope. Ah, I see. That would cut into my late-night *Halo* sessions. Well, could you do a little special one for me at, say, sevenish?"

Back to the Queen. As you know, the Marquis consoled himself about his powerlessness through his growing prowess in *Halo*, but when in the presence of someone capable of real violence, virtuosic violence, even he, deluded though he was, knew that *Halo*-power was a lot like thinking you had a steady girlfriend because you paid $5 to watch a teenager go 'round the world with a vibrator on her webcam.

But all these reasons were just background noise, like an interstellar hissing, for his real reason for dread. He was pretty sure why she was coming, and he was pretty sure it had something to do with the visit of that strange masked man a month or so back. The idea of that conversation was, in a word, terrifying.

I am not being hyperbolic when I say that the Marquis was terrified. For he had a little guilty secret, and he had a sad sinking feeling that he was about to be busted on it. His secret was this: the card that the masked man had presented to him was not blank. It had a message, all right. The message was indeed from a powerful woman in the Hebrides, the Queen of Spells, and it was a simple request that the Marquis bring his authority and influence to bear in order to get Percy registered in some sort of computer-technician program at the local community college. No doubt she thought that her request would have been taken up as a part of his routine constituent services. At the very least he should have been able to get the college to drop the out-of-state tuition.

So, for something so simple, something so obviously not requiring anything extraordinary, why had he—on the spot!—made a decision to claim that the note was blank? Well, it's an easy question to ask now, but then he thought that his little fib would play out without incident. He sure didn't foresee the sort of existential quandary that the moustachioed golem would be thrown into, getting himself lost, and for sure for sure he had no reason to think the Queen would actually care about such a self-evident dweeb. He had assumed that the letter was itself merely the Queen's own constituent service to the forlorn masked man. In short, every instinct told him that he could write this one off, dodge it, without any negative consequences. Least of all did he suspect that the Queen herself would soon appear at his threshold, her mouth full of galling questions.

But this still doesn't say anything about why he claimed that the message was blank. The short answer is that he didn't want to be bothered by yet another needy person. That is why he had a security force, after all. He had other priorities and other goals: he wanted to be a *Halo* Legend. From the first moment that he'd heard that there were such people, Legends, that they had the most famously quick reflexes and deadly accurate mastery of all forms of *Halo* weaponry, he knew that he would devote his life, his whole life, his very quintessence, to this great purpose. If he was physically stuck in a corn state, he could still be a Legend in cyberspace, in the Cloud, a great hero spoken of in only the most reverential tones in the digitally transcendent world of *Halo*. It made him teary just to think of how glorious he could soon be.

The fact that a hireling and feckless dummy like Rory could kick his ass now and into every conceivable future that did not include the amputation of his thumbs was an inconvenient fact that he simply did not allow himself to think about. And the fact that Rory, good as he very probably was, was nothing near a Legend, that, too, he ignored. So, the basic reason was the most obvious and petty: he didn't acknowledge the message because he had to tend to his vanities.

But there was another, subtler reason, to wit: he was convinced of his own impotence. In his darkest night of the soul, he felt that he could barely push the salt shaker across the table with a rigid index finger. Really, in the end, *Halo* was his last hope because in it he was only required to push buttons with his fingers. Lacking that, there was only terrified paralysis, staring into the void, a little drool gathering on a stubbly chin. Rory could have him dunked in amber and set out on the lawn, an umber icon for the peasants to hang garlands on and cry, "Miracle! Miracle!" when the Marquis's hot tears made their sad way down his cheeks.

This conviction of ultimate impotence made it obvious to him that were he to go to the admissions office at Corn Belt Community College, he would be shown the door.

"Mr. Marquis, Corn Belt does not admit, what do you call 'em, the merely human-like. No golems, no clones, no zombies, no replicants, and no astral emulations. We admit humans. Humans looking to better themselves in a difficult economy. Humans looking for job training so they can pay their mortgage, pay their taxes, and put food on the table for their children and the occasional derelict mother-in-law. I don't understand why this phantom-in-flesh would even want a job. Does he even eat? Has he been properly microchipped by the INS? You know, GPS implants are required before enrollment for out-of-state students."

"But this is what the Queen of Spells has requested for her Thing. What will I say to her? What will *you* say to her?"

A smile of industrial-strength condescension.

"Well, the Queen should know that Corn Belt Community College has its own standards and, most importantly, its own Trustee-approved procedures. This would violate procedure. Can you can please communicate that robust fact to the Queen? Surely, she will understand the concept of 'best practices' even if it's a little above your pay grade. I'm sure she consults best practices when herding the fairies, or what have you, out there in the Hebrides. By the way, where are those damned islands? Do you know?"

"What if I, your Marquis, demanded it?"

"Please, Mr. Marquis, for my sake, for your sake, don't go there. Don't take that route. Don't cop that attitude. If it helps (because it does help me), just say to yourself 'policy.' Say it over and over. Close your eyes. Take deep, even breaths, slow everything down, find inner calm, and say 'policy.'"

That was what the Marquis expected and what he was sure, correctly, he would find at dear Corn Belt: humiliation at the hands of the admissions staff. They probably wouldn't even let him talk to the head of admissions. He, after all, had real power, and lived in haughty isolation, at the end of a long sheetrocked hallway, the door guarded by a single sentry, who asked of all comers, "Who dares?"

"Policy, policy," he said to himself, closing his eyes.

I should tell you that, based on my own extensive experience, this is exactly what college bureaucrats are like, but, frankly, I never met one this articulate and self-knowing. I never met one with such a shapely and muscular philosophy. Otherwise, my feeling is that college administrators and their bureaucrats should be shot on sight like the zombies that America's youth are so fond of gunning down these days.

12.

"Tiberius complained that to be emperor was to hold a wolf by the ears."

—STRINGFELLOW BARR

Well, like any dreaded thing that one imagines so far off that it will never actually arrive, the time arrived. The Marquis and the Queen of Spells sat opposite each other in the Marquis's private chamber.

The Queen was not dressed like something out of the dank past, some darkened druidess. She was dressed in knock-off Izod and Lacoste sportswear that she had picked up just that morning, after breakfast at the Denny's restaurant at College Hills Shopping Mall. While eating a Grand Slam breakfast, she saw a TJ Maxx across Veteran's Parkway, which street, at great risk to her life, she crossed on foot. She loaded up on $10 polo shirts and $20 blue jeans, and called a taxi to get her back safely to her motel. She couldn't wait to show the sporty vestments to her pals back on the Isle of Islay, where strip malls and discount stores were a vexed fantasy.

Her Spellness was taken aback by the Marquis's room. The walls were yellowed and the paint was peeling around the heating vents. There was a large brown spot of water damage in an outside corner of the ceiling (standard feature with old galvanized plumbing). The furnishing was just a few mismatched and threadbare armchairs, and a couch so stained and sunken that not even the Marquis's matted and petulant cocker spaniel would sit on it. In the center of the room was this enormous monolithic thing over which a king-sized bed sheet had been thrown. That, we know, was the wide, wide, widescreen television console and all manner of Xbox paraphernalia. For obvious reasons, the idea that the conversation might somehow turn to *Halo* terrified the Marquis. He knew he'd break down and confess to the slaughter of the little ones, the masked man's delicate and defenseless companions. As for the TV itself, you could feel its radiant indignation at being covered as if it were something to be ashamed of. Even though its plug had been pulled, you could still see a pale glow just behind the sheet where it sulked in resentment.

The Marquis himself was dressed in the fabric of royalty, but it was tattered, as if he'd been given the stuff by a local theater company that was cleaning out its closets. ("Hey, maybe that bitch the Marquis would like this moth-eaten stuff.") Worse yet, his hair was long, oily, and uncombed. He'd shaved, but it appeared that he'd used an old razor; there were stubborn spots where you could still see a week's stubble asserting itself. As for his teeth, he was a dental hygienist's nightmare: the plaque on his lower front teeth had scaled the teeth nearly to the top, and his gums were bright red with infection. (Thus the just deserts of the hash-smoking habituated gamer.) Finally, he seemed nervous and twitchy, as if he were working on his second pot of coffee or his third dose of Benzedrine.

"Obviously," she thought to herself, "recent years have not

been kind to the American nobility. It's easy to imagine how something could go awry for Percy."

At any rate, they were seated now.

"W-w-welcome," he said, as if what he meant was "Don't hit me!"

She shifted her shoulders and turned her head, increasingly skeptical. At last she said, "Monsieur le Marquis, I have a problem, a concern, that I'm hoping you can help me with."

"F-for sure." He smiled, mean and sniveling.

"A few months ago, I sent to you a denizen of my domain. He carried with him a message. He was not strictly speaking a human, although he should easily have passed for one. He was in fact one of my little creatures, surely you've heard of them. At any rate, he has not yet returned. Did he meet with you?"

The Marquis tried to remember what he did with his face when he was thinking. He settled for the sort of expression used when looking for something that has rolled under a bed.

"Several months ago, you say?"

"Just a few. Two, maybe." She felt a little creepy on this point. She herself wondered why she had been so late in looking into the matter. The Marquis sensed it might be a weakness, something that might help to exculpate him, should push come to shove.

"That's a lot to expect of my poor old memory."

"Please try."

"Okay."

The look of trying.

"He would have been dressed all in black. And he is fond of wearing a mask like the old Zorro TV character, if you remember him. His name is Percy."

"Nope. I don't remember anyone of that description. N-nice

little name, though, I like it, especially for something n-not-quite-human. Percy, percept, persiflage, percid . . . "

"What is percid?"

"Oh, the f-family of sp-spiny freshwater fish in which one finds the p-perch."

Frown.

"No? Not heard of them?"

"Please. Also, he might have had a plastic sword."

Laughs. "Must be a cute little guy."

"So you never received him?"

"No, not that I recall." He was gaining confidence, and some of the nauseating twitches on his face and the stuttering were starting to calm and smooth out.

"Well, don't you keep a record of visitors?"

"Madame Queen of Spells, as you can see, my estate has fallen on h-hard times. Now, you might look around town and say, 'It's a prosperous little d-district, he should be doing okay with the tithes, et cetera,' but we had a little setback last year with a grand-stepdaughter, the blackened thing, and I am forced to pay down a painful second mortgage. Until I can do that, well, it's complicated. In any event, I have only one aide, Rory, and he is unhelpful. He can make a computer hum, but in all other ways he is, frankly, pretty stupid. Most Americans are like that now, although that's no excuse for Rory. But I might as well ask that stool to keep records."

This was all disappointing to the Queen, but she persevered.

"One other thing: he should have been traveling with a large number of little men with little horses. They were keeping his spirits up. Perhaps you saw them."

Of course, the Marquis remembered quite clearly his happy evening of indiscriminate slaughter. Frankly, he was sorry there weren't more such little men and many more such evenings. He knew too well that when Rory and the others had turned the masked man out, there was not a horsebacked companion left.

He blushed, grew rigid, started to sweat. He looked down, illogically fearing that the little bodies might be piled at his feet like wounded birds. Pulling himself together, he offered this: "N-now that you mention these little men, I do recall R-rory saying something about a strange man who knocked at the door one night. As I recall, the man said that he had committed an atrocity. Perhaps the atrocity he referred to had s-something to do with the little men."

"Your man R-rory says this?"

"No, R-rory."

"R-rory."

"Never m-mind."

Well, that was all she was going to listen to. The Marquis was a self-serving liar. For God's sake, she knew her own creature and he was no ruffian, and he certainly wouldn't slaughter the Queen's cheerful leprechauns (for that's what they were for all intents and purposes). Percy knew better than that. It was the Marquis himself who seemed uncomfortable, guilty-like, about her little men. She was getting a clearer idea of what had happened.

As she walked out onto the Marquis's driveway, she saw something glinting under a shrub. It was one of the little plastic swords. She picked it up and held it up for the Marquis to look at. He chuckled and put his hand to his mouth as if to say "whoops." She understood now that she would have to find Percy on her own, without the help of the Marquis. But she made a note: when she did find him, she would return to the Marquis, and then he would learn what her great powers were all about. She looked forward to it.

She knew something now, or thought she did, about the fate

of her little men on horseback. Her brow came fiercely together between her eyes, as if it were a spearhead. It wasn't enough evidence to hang him on just yet, but as a token of the vengeance she would one day take, she conjured a deluge of black slugs and other slimy critters, including newts and the small aquatic or semiaquatic urodele amphibians of the family Salamandridae, ankle deep in the Marquis's chamber.

She stood in his circular drive (with its pompous aqueous-green glazed tiles imported from Dresden, and the equally flamboyant weeds that swaggered in the cracks), and listened for his scream. She smiled when it came, because it was even more miserable than she'd hoped for.

13.

"We are again confronted with one of the most vexing aspects of advanced industrial civilization: the rational character of its irrationality."

—MARCUSE

—after Jonathan Swift

When the Queen of Spells left the Marquis, it was clear to her that she would not get any help from him or anyone else in this strange place. She was on her own. She would have to provide her own resources, and fortunately, as we have seen, she was not lacking in them. The first thing she did, in order to make her task manageable, was to reduce the town to the size of a shoe-box. In this fashion she was able to lift it, turn it this way and that, get the lay of the land, so to speak, peek in a few windows, and generally satisfy herself that she knew the place.

It should not surprise you to learn, knowing what you already know of this odd middle-western town, N—, that most of the townsfolk found their new tiny reality excessively "liberal." Organizations were formed, protests planned, and the "Bigger Party" was formed, offering a list of candidates for city council and mayor. But many business and civic leaders found the new tiny reality interesting, as they themselves expressed it. A banner was strung across Main Street encouraging people to "Celebrate the New Interesting." Inevitably, the local college students seized on this as an encouragement to party, and in short order the celebration became one of their infamous beer riots.

It could have been a lot worse. The students generated leaders (as a swamp will spawn frogs) and a Facebook page for the party was created. Students from all over the state were invited for the "biggest, baddest" keg-fest ever. One can only imagine the disappointment when the out-of-town revelers, having driven all the way from Carbondale and Charleston and Macomb, discovered that N— was only a lively shoebox. After some consideration, the out-of-town revelers concluded, "Whatever, man!" and drank their beer by the side of the road, amusing themselves—*and it was funny!*—by flattening the little town and using it as a Frisbee.

Fortunately, by the second day the students had emptied all the kegs, returned home, and collapsed back into their sodden apartments after which the more balanced opinion of the adults came to the fore. At a memorable meeting of the town council, residents complained that the new town felt "cramped." The mayor said that he understood their complaint, but they should acknowledge that there were very positive payoffs for the new downsized municipality, and folks needed to take them into consideration. For example, he offered, property taxes would essentially disappear since the largest estate in town now could be covered by a postage stamp. And most city services could be eliminated since they could now cut the grass at the park with Granny Osage's pinking shears, and the thimbleful of garbage they'd generate each week could simply be dumped outside of their town-box, into the old big world, where it would be no larger than an average sparrow poop. I don't need to tell you how persuasive these ideas were for these simple people. They were all for it.

Sadly, all of these arguments became moot when the city's liability lawyer observed that many people had been taken to the emergency ward at local hospitals because of various bumps and bruises suffered as the Queen turned her toy town this way and that (not to mention the calamities they all suffered while being thrown around like a Frisbee). He said that if the town in any way recognized the New Interesting as settled law, the town would face multiple liability suits for damages to person and property that would drive it into bankruptcy.

A disappointed "Oh!" filled the room, and one thin graybeard angrily complained that, "Federal regulators should keep their hands off our freedom to be as tiny as we want!"

This mooting was made even mootier because the Queen of Spells decided that she'd learned what she needed to know about the place, and, having no intention of shrinking herself, she returned N— to its accustomed scale, and to its time-honored grievances with reality.

14.

*"[To read a bad novel] is to yield your imagination for hours
to people with whom, face to face, you would be ashamed to
exchange even a few words."*

—SCHLEGEL

Once N— had been returned to its just proportions, our Queen
of Spells set one foot before the other and began her quest. And
to every person she met she asked the same strangled question,
"Have you seen a young masked man yclept 'Percy'?"

Sadly, each of her interrogators had the same reply: "What's
'yclept'?"

After a few days of fruitless searching, she found herself
walking through a campus of WPA-style brick buildings. Seeing more raccoons than people, she concluded that this place
was abandoned, and began to walk toward the next neighborhood over. But then she saw a man sitting on a long, covered
porch painting a portrait of a young woman. He was dressed all
in worn white linen, and he wore a blond hat woven from fine
fibers. She went to him, dogged in her purpose.

I won't say he was happy to be disturbed, but he was cordial
about it, and asked if she would like to sit with him in the shade
of the porch. She happily accepted his offer. After all, walking
in a built-to-scale N— was tiring. It was clear to our always
pellucid Queen that this was a charming man, very Old World
in an iconoclastic way.

"Can I get you a cup of coffee?" he asked.

"I would be so grateful if you could."

When he entered his studio, she had time to look at the painting he was working on. It was of a beautiful young woman in a

loose, airy blouse. He had a small photograph of her clipped to the easel. Her hair was cut very short, and she affected a certain haughty harshness: a tiny silver dagger pierced the upper part of her ear. The Queen noticed that the figure was seen through a sepia wash that suggested certain familiar, if unnamed, earthy difficulties. The painting itself seemed to be as much about this tension—a lovely harshness—as it was about the figure as such. All of this the artist captured intuitively, dreamily, yet articulately, in the painting.

He returned with the coffee and asked her Spellness who she was and why she was here. When she told him that she was a fairy Queen from the Isle of Islay, he said, "No lie?"

She told him that she was on a search, and then she asked her forlorn question.

He responded, "What's 'yclept'?"

She sighed. Damn it, she was a *fairy queen* after all! How else was she to put it! She was loath to dumb down her diction, which was, she well knew, nothing less than proper, appropriate, and in every way correct. Americans!

"Listen, a little piece of advice," the artist said, "don't say 'yclept' anymore. People around here won't like it. I'm sorry if that disappoints you. Just say that you're looking for Percy. You'll get better results."

She stared at him. She was wondering if this conversation and everything she had experienced in this strange place, this N—, weren't also something shrouded in a sepia wash, just like his painting.

"Well, however you want to put it, your Percy shouldn't be too hard to find. Everyone knows him or knows of him, although it's not surprising that our townsfolk aren't eager to admit it. But let me be sure: it's the Zorro-lookin' guy that you're searching for, right?"

She nearly jumped from her chair. At last! "Yes, yes he is! He wears a little mask."

"That's him, although he lost the mask some time back."

"Please tell me more!"

He frowned. "I'm not sure you're going to like this story, given what I know about it. But I'm not the one to tell it. It's not my place and not my business. Keep asking around, just as you're doing now. You'll find him. He sure isn't trying not to be found." Laughter. "Why, almost everyone in town has found him at one time or another."

15.

Fellini: My work can't be anything other than a testimony of what I am looking for in life. It is a mirror of my searching.
Playboy: Searching for what?
Fellini: For myself freed.

THE BORSALINO: A ROMANCE

After Felicité had ended her conversation with the artist and gone on her troubled way, I walked over from my catbird seat behind a garden wall and asked him a few questions, just for background.

"Background? What kind of background?" he asked. He seemed just a little annoyed at all the interruptions that morning.

"In my experience, it always helps to be able to provide convincing detail. This painting you're working on, for example, and the photograph of this vivid woman that is clipped to it. That sort of thing can make all the difference in delivering a scene. For instance, one thing that I'm thinking now, looking forward in my narrative, is that the hat you are wearing might make a compelling detail."

"My hat?"

"I'm sure you understand this. Say you're painting this woman and you decide to put a vase of flowers near her."

"I don't paint flowers."

"That's not the point."

It occurred to me just then that he had not offered me coffee.

"Look. I'd just like to know what you call that hat. Does it have a name? Could you perhaps call it a boater? It would be thrilling to me if I could call it a boater."

"It's a Borsalino."

"A Borsalino. Not bad. I can use that."

"Look here," he said, "do you see this tag? It says '11.' That means grade 11 in their line of hats. A grade-11 Borsalino retails for six hundred and fifty dollars."

"Do tell."

"Would you like to know how much I paid for it? One twenty-five."

"Hell of a deal."

"The grades go up into the forties. Do you know how much a Borsalino in the forties costs? As much as six thousand dollars."

"Wow."

"I have always wondered what kind of person would pay that much for a hat."

"Frankly, I don't know anyone who would pay a hundred and twenty-five dollars for a hat. Or twenty-five. But I run with a cheap crowd."

He looked dumbfounded, if you like that sort of Germanized word mongrel. He eyed me skeptically, wondering if I was "putting him on," as people once said.

He continued. "You might also like to know that this particular Borsalino has a name."

"Nice. The name has a name. This is getting better."

"It is a Monte Cristo."

He gave the name an Italian lilt of the kind you might imagine coming from someone who was born just up the interstate in Kankakee: *MON*-te *CREE*-sto. Frankly, he sounded more like Bela Lugosi than any Italian I'd ever meet.

"You can tell it's a Monte Cristo by the fold in the top of the hat."

"That's more than I need to know. This is not a novel about a hat."

"Look, if you're going to include a hat in your story, especially my hat, you should know what you're talking about. *This* is a Borsalino. A Monte Cristo Borsalino. Now, as you can see from the fine, soft weave of the material, if you wanted you could fold it, and, in fact, Europeans do fold it."

He said "Europeans" as if they were a very special species of human.

"They fold it and put it in this little bag"—he took a velvety cloth bag from his pocket—"so that it can be carried just as you would carry an umbrella. The little cloth bag with the cotton drawstring is so precious in itself that . . . I mean, it's beautiful."

"I understand."

"Isn't it cool?"

"Very cool."

16.

THE BORSALINO: A ROMANCE, PARTE DUE

Then he turned his back to me. He reached up, slowly, as if he reached for a small child who had been riding on his shoulders, and he took the Borsalino in his hands, carefully holding it by the brim. Then he placed it before us in the middle of the table, as if it were a vase containing a bouquet of bright fall marigolds.

Looking at it, perfect, with no responsibility other than being the hat that it was, tears came to my eyes, speculative tears. It seemed as though I'd known this man, and his hat, since the beginning of time.

"This hat of yours," I said, "I think it is an invitation to secret knowledge. It sits there like a portal to universal harmony."

He shook his head. "No," he said, "even though you understand, you are not quite right. The beauty of the hat is in its imbalance."

I looked back at him in surprise and perfect sincerity. "Please, what is your understanding of the happiness of the hat?"

He sat then, as if descending into a poignant daydream, and passed me a delicate china coffee cup. It was bone white, with raised flowers of purplish blue. (English, not Wedgwood but Adderley.) The blue seeped just beyond the flower as if it were a watercolor on paper. Holding it, I found that the cup was as fragile as the skull of some infant saint. The hat was sacred, but the cups, too, were now sacred. Everything had the bluish-green glow of the Other Side. I thought with wonder, "Is everything he touches sacred?"

He smiled with understanding at the sincerity of my thought and said, "That's enough discussion. Let's have some coffee."

Finally!

17.

"Do all humans have to be human beings?"

—NOVALIS

But Percy, dear Percy.

You know, he was not really as you think of him now, a mere grotesque that has stumbled out of the night and into our lives. He was more than a perverse mannequin with a crotch like smooth plaster. He had his own subjectivity, his own inmost reality, and it is high time that we begin to discover it.

Putting aside for the moment our uncertainty about what exactly Percy is—a machine like Hoffmann's Coppelia? A stone ignited into obtuse life like Pygmalion? A pure conjuration like something Manfred could summon? Or, applying Occam's razor, just another suffering human like you?—all that aside, when he was shown the door by Rory and his pals, and he stood before the empty cobblestones in the Marquis's courtyard, and he heard the clattering echoes of things past racketing like falling rocks, meaninglessly, and he lifted his head up toward the vacuum of space, he was actually a very simple thing: he was lonely.

He himself had no idea who or what he was. He remembered, certainly, that there had been a sort of mother, the Queen, who had sent him thither, waving a hanky and weeping like mothers ought. At first, her image offered him consolation, but now he felt angry resentment as he thought to himself, "I wish I'd never been born. If that's even what it was! Was I born? I feel worthless and I'd happily kill myself if I knew how to do it." (I loosely render these thoughts for the convenience of my reader in order to avoid the impression that we are merely looking at the inner workings of something numb and dumb, like looking into the eye of a cow.)

It's easy to sympathize with his feelings. He'd started out with such confidence and optimism, although he would not have known what those words mean. But people who feel that they have been assigned a duty, who have been sent out on a mission by a Great Person, will do what is required even if they can't explain it all, or even a little. Duty is duty, loyalty loyalty. Moreover, he was given courage by his companions. How well he remembered the little men on their horses, with their pennants and standards, neatly lined up behind him like the terra cotta armies that once stood behind the emperor Qin Shi Huang. How could he not have felt stout-hearted? Fearless, bold, intrepid, resolute, and super-manly? He had spunk. He had sand and grit in his makeup. And backbone, forsooth.

But where were they now, his little comrades? They certainly weren't here in the courtyard where he'd left them. The Marquis's horrible suggestion that he'd slaughtered them all while playing some sort of game made no sense and sickened him. One thing seemed clear: he couldn't return home to the Queen without some sort of explanation.

"Where are all of your friends? Your brothers in arms?" she'd ask.

"I don't know."

"You don't know? How can you not know? Sit down, mister.

I want an explanation. Now, there were a lot of them, and I asked you to look out for them, didn't I?"

"I thought they were taking care of me."

"Don't you try to place the blame on those poor little guys!"

"And don't you just render them back into flabby cack when they return?"

"Wherever did you get such an idea?"

"The cack master told me."

"Well, I shall have a word with him as well. But you won't distract me. What, did you just leave them over there with those horrid Americans? They are probably living in Sacramento, in one of those homeless encampments by that disconsolate river. They are listening to the squalid cackling of bag ladies, pushing around shopping carts full of worn shoes. They are covering their innocent ears at night when the smelly trollops are brutalized over and over by fermenting hobos."

"What is fermenting?"

"Did you at least make sure that they applied for food stamps?"

"What are food stamps?"

"Oh! You should be ashamed of yourself. Go to your room!"

"I don't have a room."

"Well, then just go."

Tears came just thinking about the possibility of this scene.

Of course, the Queen of Spells would have said no such thing, although Percy is not to be blamed for not knowing that. This is what she'd have said. She'd have said, "It's okay, sweetheart, calm down. They were just little creatures that I made to keep you company. Each one began as a little bit of spit and a single breath. They were no more than bubbles."

Ah, there was the rub.

"But dear Queen, dear author, what then am I?"

18.

"Only that which is the abyss of meaning can be at the same time the ground of it."

—PAUL TILLICH

Except for the black mask, the stingy-brimmed fedora, and the fine calfskin gloves, Percy was much like any other homeless person in the first decades of the twenty-first century. Oh, and the tight, tight black leather pants that shaped his buttocks in a particularly buttery way. That was different too. It may surprise you that I call attention to his pants and ass now, after all we've been through, now when he is so lost and vulnerable. If it does surprise you, it won't for long.

To say that Percy didn't have a place to stay is to state the obvious. It's not as if the Queen had given him a credit card so that he could stay at a motel. Who knows what she had been thinking? Maybe she assumed that the Marquis would put him up, or let him do some couch surfing among the local aristocracy. He was, as usual, clueless about her intentions.

That first night, he just walked. (SOP among the newly homeless.) He walked from the Marquis's manor over to Linden, then south to Eastland Mall, where he found a half-eaten bag of caramel popcorn on the ground in front of a J.Jill outlet. He didn't much like it, but he ate it. (The Queen had him on a whole-grain, plant-based diet back in the old country.) Then he walked across Veterans Parkway, where he was narrowly missed by cars in every lane. Exhausted, he sat among the enormous concrete blocks left behind where the old Holiday Inn had been torn down. The blocks seemed to him like the last traces of a once-proud civilization that was no more. He half-expected to see the giant head of some dead king, some Ozymandias, rolled to the side with these crapulous concrete slabs.

The next night he concluded that he really did need to find a place to sleep, so he walked over to a nearby subdivision, Collie Ridge Estates. (No collies, ridges, or estates have ever been sighted anywhere near Collie Ridge Estates.) There he found a Chrysler SUV, got in, watched *Spider-Man 2* on the backseat video player, and curled up for sleep beneath a blanket with Shrek on it. "This isn't so bad," he thought in the full innocence of his heart.

As you might imagine, the SUV was not a permanent solution. He was awakened the next morning by an adolescent girl, mouth bulging with an erector set of finely laced metal, a set of designer braces modeled after the Golden Gate Bridge, *haute monde* among N—'s teens.

The girl said, as best she could, "Hey, Mom, the Joker is sleeping in the backseat of the car." That's the closest approximation I can give of what she said, because it really sounded a lot like a teaspoon stuck in a garbage disposal.

"Who?"

"The Joker."

"The Joker! Honey, the Joker is not a real person."

"OMG, you know who he looks like? Kelsey posted a picture of a guy like this on her Facebook page. Only this guy's still got his pants on."

"What?!" She looked in and was struck with awe. "Honey, do you know who that is? It's Zorro! And just why is Kelsey posting pictures of men with their pants off?"

She ignored her mother's question. "Maybe she's trying to share him with me."

Blinding metallic flash of lecherous teenage incisors.

To make a long story short, eventually the police explained

to Percy the downside of sleeping in other people's SUVs. Percy was disappointed. He rather liked the teenaged girl, in spite of the fact that she made his ears ring when she talked. The girl, her name was Melissa, or Missy, suggested that if Percy couldn't sleep in the SUV, he could sleep in her room, but when he nodded his head in agreement there was such a righteous clamor from her mother and the police that, with yet another disconsolate sigh, he gave up on the idea.

For her part, the girl pitched a fit, saying, "Please, Mommy! Please! He'll be quiet! He can just sleep on the rug by the closet." Then, "I never get anything I want! I hate you!"

"Forget it. You are not sleeping with Zorro."

"Who is Zorro?" Percy asked.

Later, he was driven to the outer walls of the city where muscular men—wearing skintight Under Armour sleeveless T's, tattoos of jungle vines and blossoms spilling down their arms—rolled open the city gates. One of them pointed beyond the gates and said, "That is where the dogs sleep, in that field of grass across the road. You should join them. It's where you belong." As Percy passed, they performed bodybuilder poses that inflated their tattoos and caused the vines to pulse with menacing snakes and panthers in the undergrowth.

Percy spent the day sharing smells with his new comrades, and woke the next morning in a tousy shag of warm fur. The dogs were sympathetic about his predicament, and why not? They were not so different. He was grateful to them, but, at the same time, he couldn't help feeling a little depressed that his lustrous black regalia was now dull and covered with dog fur.

His situation was bad. He did not really know what or where N— was. He didn't know what an Illinois was. He didn't know if there were more hospitable places nearby. So, he could stay with the dogs, be with them at the Dumpsters where the fast-food joints flung down their excess burgers and chicken-like portions. He could shit on the ground with them, sleep in the dog-dark night, and, at dawn, join in singing their doggy plainsongs and chants. Or, he could sweep the fur, the grease, and the vague, wild smell of piss and bile from his swell black getup and get back into town. The dogs all said he was a human, and that he should go back inside and make the best of it. This fragrant field of balms and attendant bees was no place for him. But just beware of the coppers. They didn't like dogs and they obviously didn't like him.

He replied, sadly, "Okay, I'll go. But are you sure I'm human?"

That thought was way too heavy for the dogs, who lacked proper preparation for Kant's "transcendental deduction." A couple of the older, grouchier dogs, who thought they knew it all, growled unpleasantly, thinking that our Percy was perhaps a wisenheimer, as they put it. (They were what you might call love-it-or-leave-it dogs, and they wanted him to go back where he came from. Actually, I think they just said, "Git!")

Anyway, back through the city gates he went, without much hope, half-thinking that he should have just bared his throat to the jingoistic canines. As for the gatekeepers, they didn't seem to recognize him. They handed him coupons for an oil change and a thirty-six-point vacation checkup, a two-fer-one at Boo-boo's Chicago Style Dog House, and special introductory rates at one of those newfangled ChakraBump soul studios where they do cross training in the front with a retired drill sergeant, and massage in the back where the girls wait their turn, mar-garitas in hand. Sort of like basic combat training joined to a gay bathhouse.

But there was still the problem of sleeping arrangements for our hero. Where would *you* have slept? His only thought was that he should sleep where there were beds, and the beds were in houses, so he'd just go to houses and ask if they had a free bed for the evening. As you might imagine, simple as it sounded to him, this didn't work out well, and had the unfortunate consequence of bringing the "coppers" back into the picture. Happily, the dogs had instructed him well in "running away." Most nights, the best he could do was wait for lights-out, and then make himself at home on a chaise longue out in the backyard. One morning when the owner, I think her name was Wanda, came out to sunbathe, drink her a.m. piña colada, and comb her platinum-blond hair, she felt the weird shift in magnetic fields caused by the fairie creature sleeping on her patio. And when she saw Percy in his lubricious leather jeans, she hummed, "Hmmm."

Wanda's hum would prove fateful, at least for the next forty-five minutes.

Lacking an alternative, Percy kept at it, knowing that he didn't need the offer of a bed in every house he asked at, just one. Just one lucky house. And thus it was that, early one evening, he found that one.

It was a decent if somewhat worn tract home with the nicest sort of vinyl-covered aluminum porch rails. A woman answered the door, plump but attractive in a softly glowing kind of way. He could tell there was something different about her as soon as she appeared, silhouetted by a corona thrown upon her by a huge flat-screen monitor in the background. When she saw Percy, her mouth dropped in mixed astonishment and awe. She said, "He is come. The one I was told of." She went to her knees and bathed his feet with her tears.

Then she said, "Your place here is ready. My name is Fanni.

I have been waiting for you." She rose and took his hand, like Beatrice leading her beloved Pilgrim to that place where God's ways are explained to man, to that place where willing and doing are one.

19.

"Every authentic work of art has one primary purpose: to find what it means to be a work of art."

—SCHLEGEL

Just as Percy had done in his search for a bed, Felicité went door to door, saying, "Hello, have you seen this young man?" just as if she were looking for a lost cat. "His name is Percy and he may have been wearing a mask."

Weirdly, no one had a neutral response. No one said, "Nope. Sorry." Some had a look of horror and said nothing. Others cried aloud and slammed the door shut. A few said, "Oh, my God, Percy! If you find him, please tell me. I can't go on like this. I'll give you twenty dollars. I'll give you my car, whatever it takes. Here's my cellphone number. Call me!"

Finally, late in the first morning of her quest, a man answered her knocks. He had mascara tattooed around his eyes, as if he worshipped Nefertiti, and a large image of the sun above the outside corner of his right eye shedding its beneficent rays across his face. (Apparently, he fancied Akhenaten's Amarna style for his tattoos.) He took the photo, gave it a quick look, and said, "Hey, that's Percy."

"You know him?"

He smiled, slyly, "Well, everybody knows him."

"Do you know where he might be?"

"Oh, I know where he *is*. Eh, you see that house at the end of the cul-de-sac?"

"With the white porch rails."

"Yeah, the one that's got the carved newel post."

"Yes. I see it. That is amazingly . . . "

"Phallic."

"Yes . . ."

"Well, just go there and ask. He's been living in that house with Fanni and her boyfriend. Real fixture in the neighborhood now."

"My God, how wonderful! I've found him!"

"Wonderful? Are you really sure you want this Percy?"

"Of course I am. I'm his mother."

"Really!? Nothing personal, but you don't look like his kind, let alone his mother. Frankly, I've never thought of Percy as a person with a mother."

"What can you mean?"

The tattooed sun above his right eye flared uncomfortably. It seemed that it might burn him.

"I apologize. It's nothing. Forgive me. Anyway, if you go down there, just give him a little peck on the cheek for me and say, 'Gerald will see you Thursday at seven o'clock.'"

"You will not see him Thursday because he's returning this afternoon with me to his home in the Hebrides."

"The Hebrides? Oh, so you're . . . "

"The Queen of Spells."

"Of course! Hey, where the hell are the Hebrides? They're islands, right?"

Looking a little exasperated and impatient to be on her way, she just glared at him.

"Oh, never mind, I'll Google it. But one last thing before

you go. You're not the first person to suggest that Percy needs to leave town. You're the first mother, of course, but not the first person. Like you, they all say they want to help him, or it's for his own good, or our good, or whatever. Some have even complained that his 'methods are unsound,' whatever that means. I've never found anything lacking in his methods. Frankly, I've never seen any method at all. But, as you can see, he is not gone. That's part his doing and part ours. You see, we love Percy here, in our own way. He has his perfect place not merely in our midst but in our very hearts, dark though they may be. You might even say that he is venerated.

"When you go down there, you will meet another person. Her name is Fanni, but don't let that give you the wrong impression. There's nothing soft about her when it comes to Percy. She is like the pope of Percy, or something. I don't know how to put it. If you ask her, she'll explain that there was the One who was given up by his followers in the garden at Gethsemane, and there is this One, and his name is Percy. That famous betrayal, Fanni says, will not happen again, not on her watch. This probably doesn't make much sense to you, but then you're a pagan, aren't you?"

20.

"I follow the law of the good only in so far as it is compatible with undisturbed sensual pleasure."

—KARL JASPERS

Felicité walked up to the house that Gerald had pointed to. When she came to the newel post, she regarded it carefully, and circled the palm of her hand speculatively above its tumescent head. Instantly, there was a snap of electricity and a rainbow of intense hues hovered between her hand and the post. She pulled her hand back.

"So," she observed, "there is Power here."

She knocked on the door and it was answered promptly.

It was Percy.

"Mother!"

"My child!"

She took him in her arms.

Quickly up behind him came a woman—Fanni, as we now know—cleanly dressed in a nice summer outfit that was belted at the waist and printed with red hedge roses. She was smiling, and she seemed full of an organic friendliness. She was like the idea of a mother that you would get from someone else's mother, not your own.

"Who is it, Percy?" Fanni asked.

"It's my mother. Sort of."

Felicité and Percy soon requested, and were granted, a private place where they could talk. Percy took her hand and led her to a cheerful, sunny room overlooking a beautiful and carefully maintained garden. Whoever kept it knew and appreciated the difference between a flower and a weed. They sat at a small table and Fanni brought them cups of tea—smoky Russian Caravan—and a vase of freshly picked flowers, mostly lilies and purple coneflower, all from the spotless garden.

Her Spellness looked into the heart of a coneflower, with its bright yellow-brown seeds spiking out in stellar order, just as it was in the beginning.

"Percy, I can't tell you how worried I've been. But it's all right now, I've come to take you home."

Percy squirmed.

"Mother, if that's what you are to me . . ."

"You've always called me mother!" She was genuinely surprised and a little hurt by the way Percy put it.

" . . . a few short days ago, or so it seems, nothing could have made me happier than to leave this strange place and return to our enchanted home. But now this is my home. I belong here. I know that will sound strange to you, but here I am not just some ill-wrought extension of yourself, a dirty growth on your thigh, a suspicious lump that a doctor would look at and say, 'Hmmm. That doesn't look good.' Here I am quite real, maybe even realer than real." He laughed. "I'm too real for my own good, I know that!"

The Queen's eyes were at the same time confused and moist with sadness.

"Oh, Percy! I don't understand what you're saying!"

"What I'm saying is that I have a purpose here. I do things that contribute to the spiritual health of the commonwealth. People come here ardent, as if committed to an ancient religious duty. I never sought any of this. I was just looking for a place to sleep. But now I cannot abandon it lightly."

The Queen peered at him skeptically.

"Percy, that sounds like piffle to me. Can you give me an example of what you are talking about?"

"Easily. A short walk from here lives a young man named Little Prison Face."

"That's not a nice name!"

"It was on the order of a nickname that stuck because he burned down his daddy's house with his real name, with his daddy in it. I don't know what the fuss was about. After all, his daddy was already dead. Friedrich, or Baby Fred, they called him then, before the Little Prison Face moniker. Baby Fred was his daddy-killing/house-burning name."

"Oh!"

"Later he was called Irrational Number because while Little Prison Face was doing time, he took the trouble to interrogate time's paradoxes as he discovered them through a book, *Great Ideas for Lifers*, he had found in the prison library. In this book he was introduced to Zeno, through whom he learned that the paradoxes of time could only be expressed by irrational numbers. Such numbers were depressing for him because the math seemed to suggest that his release time would never arrive. Since he had nothing but time on his hands, along with his father's blood, he began a project that could never be finished, namely: an encyclopedic account of all possible versions of Zeno's paradox. Needless to say, he soon saw that his project itself was a paradox because there is no end of the variations on Zeno's paradox."

Percy continued, "For Little Prison Face, paradox was not a solution. He was in prison. So he steeled himself to the task at hand: restore time's arrow to its rightful place, putting one thing before the other until Beginnings and Ends were fully restored and he could get out of prison. So he speculated that the two paradoxes—Zeno's and his own—cancelled each other. Unfortunately, he only succeeded in proving that the study of the paradox of Zeno's paradox was itself paradoxical. In other words, and this is what drove him to me, the study of infinity is itself infinite. And, it goes without saying, the infinity of the study of infinity was also infinite. And so on into the smoggy distance."

"Thus the criminal mind!"

"Believe it or not, this course of study had a strong influence on the parole board. They called it evidence of his 'ideational maturation.' And they let him out."

"This can't be right. Even in these awful United States, this can't be right."

"Anyway, there was a reason that Little Prison Face was in prison. He shot his father—a right-wing cult leader with a loyal and vibrant following in Decatur—in the temple—the temple of his head—with a thirty-eight, as he slept on the family couch after a long night of Jew-baiting, singing the old songs about niggers and love for the *Führer*, and Monday Night football."

"How awful!"

"He hadn't intended to shoot his 'daddums' that day, but everything just fell into place and so he said, 'Hmmm, I guess I can do this now.'"

"Percy, is this story necessary?"

"Later, he explained it all quite simply, in a straightforward manner, in all honesty, speaking in all candor . . . "

"*Percy!*"

" . . . he explained to the police that, 'This father-son thing had to come to an end.'"

"Okay. This is all very interesting, but what has it to do with you?"

"Well, Baby Fred, a.k.a. Little Prison Face, a.k.a. Irrational Number, is one of my clients. He has become dependent on my therapy. He has made a solemn promise not to wrap a lamp cord around anyone's neck, not to shoot anyone while they're sleeping, not to burn down any buildings, not to 'fug it,' a general catch-all term he uses for other forms of malevolence, and to stop his research into infinity and related mayhem so long as we are working together and making progress. And you know what? He has stuck to that commitment and is well on his way to a well-adjusted and responsible life. I even dare to call him a simple 'Fred' now and then. And now he's getting a certificate in massage and aromatherapy!

"The point is that the service I provide is clearly a health-giving benefit for the community. I wouldn't go so far as to call myself a mental-health professional, but the effect is similar. And that is the point I am making. Making for you. It is why I cannot and must not go back to careless Innisfree."

Obviously, this all perplexed our Queen.

"I think I should know, and better than you, what it is that you *are*. You are my child, or, if you insist, my creature. It doesn't matter one way or the other, I care for you in either case. But if you possess certain talents it is because I, not the people of this quaint little vinyl gulag, gave them to you, and, frankly, none of what you have been describing sounds familiar. So what is it, exactly, that you do for these people, murderers aside? Of what does your therapy consist?"

"Well, it changes from time to time. In fact, so far no two sessions have been the same. So I can only give you instances, or what Fanni likes to call 'iterations.' She's a real philosopher, you know."

"But what is it that you *do*?"

"For instance, Theodore, or Ted as he likes to be called, and his wife Trudy, or Tru, came over—she's quite beautiful, I think, especially her jugs, as Ted calls them. Anyway, Trudy got things started by asking Ted to vent his wrath on his heritage. You can tell who wears the pants in that family, when they're wearing pants. Then they crisscrossed the white ground of my fertile vector with nonfatal mammalian blood. Then she instructed Ted to put on the bony backtowards, which he did, and then laid it on thick."

"Laid what on? Laid it on what?"

"The bony backtowards, of course, and on me, of course."

"I don't understand."

"Hang on. Then Ted said that the strength of the burden-bearer, that would also be me, was failing. I was, a little bit, failing. Then he observed that there was much rubbish. He proposed to clear the rubbish by laying his jeweled pederect on Trudy's scuppered vellum. She seemed to like that and I was fine with it. I was encouraged to watch clinically, to take notes, but also to be ready when 'your time has come,' as Trudy always puts it.

"For sure they wanted to transition to something more dimensional and temporizing, specifically, the singing comforts of the man who is made of glass, and then the final ascendance of the Fury of the Oppressed. Unfortunately, it was near the top of the hour and I needed to clean up for my next appointment, and we needed to make sure the digital recorders were re-synced and the archives given proper serial numbers. I mean, it's bookkeeping, yes, but we do it at the end of every hour. But did they understand? No. Finally, Fanni came to the door, caught my eye, and pointed meaningfully to her watch.

"Trudy was still not happy about it and blamed Ted for taking so long with the bony backtowards I told you about. She complained that she hadn't gotten what she needed out of the session. She said, and I quote, 'My needs have not been met.' I said that there would be more sessions, but she said, 'I'll be back!' It sounded a little threatening, to be honest with you."

"My God, Percy, these people are deranged."

"You really think so? Why?"

"And you say all of your sessions are like this?"

"No. I said that they were like this in different ways. There are tricks of the trade to create this sense of difference when there's really not much. This usually involves hedging, dodging, and scheming, as well as the plentiful use of temporal caesura."

"How could you stand it, never knowing what personal violation the next hour might bring?"

"I don't know what you mean by 'violation.' I have never felt violated. In fact, I haven't even felt like a person. I'm not even sure that I know what these words could mean for a creature like me. You have made me so permeable that there's really not much to violate. Unless I've missed something along the way."

The Queen frowned and acknowledged, "Yes, that's true. Permeability was part of my design work. But that does not give them leave to treat my art as if it were a hydraulic sex doll!"

"And as for ritual abasement, that, I must say, has always felt very natural to me, very proper to my being. And, to be honest, there was a handsome something in it for me. I mean, just look how I thrive here!" He swept his hands grandly about the cramped room with its sterile IKEA furniture.

"But, you know," Percy said, his eyes moist with emotion, "none of these stories that shock you so much really captures the heart of the matter. In the end, what it is that they love in me—*love*, I say, Mother—is that I am like a nerve over which creep the otherwise unfelt cruelties of the world."

21.

"We touch heaven when we lay our hands on a human body."

—NOVALIS

"How many of these sessions do you have in a day?" asked Felicité, decorous and attentive once again.

"Oh, my schedule is full. As we speak, Fanni is negotiating a new time for the Andersons. They'll be upset, of course. The next available time is in a month, barring cancellations. It's like trying to get in to see your psychiatrist. But I hope they'll understand. After all, how often does my mother come to visit?"

"Indeed."

"Anyway, we can only talk for a few more minutes. Fanni stresses customer service."

"How much do you charge these disturbing people?"

"Oh, there is no charge. But we do encourage tithing, and folks are generally quite happy with that arrangement, especially since they'll want another appointment. Fanni's calendar makes contracts unnecessary. Fanni says that we get about five percent of our client's after-tax annual income."

"Do you get any of this money?"

"What would I do with money? I already have a bed to sleep in."

"Buy a plane ticket home?"

"Mother, please."

"Oh, I'm very unhappy. I'm not used to seeing my creations treated like this. I'm on the verge of invoking a mother's wrath."

"Whatever you've got, Fanni's up for it. Just remember, I'm the closest thing to compassion most of these folks have ever known."

"This is vexing."

"As your pal the Marquis said to me, 'You look at things in the way people do.' I think he meant that that was a problem, and I believe him now, I see his point. *You* are looking at things in the way people do. But it's so simple: all of the things people say are simply the things that they say. There's no good or bad in any of it. They mean well, I think, in some general sense, but that doesn't matter. Am I making any sense?"

The Queen of Spells was spellbound.

"Let me try another way."

Suddenly he grew agitated, as if things were not entirely lovely for him in this place in spite of all claims to the contrary.

"The only problem that I have is that I can't wake up. People say that life is a dream, and I'd really like to be here with you, even if it is in a dream. You know? People here used to say I was a gift, but not a gift in good taste. But, again, that's just one of those things that people say, and what we're trying to do is we're trying to cure them of their sayings. That's what we do here. Cure people of the things they say. In theory, once we have cured them, both sincerity and irony will have dissolved just as a bank of fog rolls in the embrace of a lake. That will be the end of the things we say, and good riddance, for then we will only have what is."

"Percy, you're getting a little carried away."

"Listen, Mother, we seek something so simple, and we seek it by ridding, by ripping out, the Law of What is Said from their hearts! Only then can my people, in all their unhappiness, say something that is not a tyrannous platitude. And in that moment of freedom from 'How It Must Be Done,' they are for a moment, a sliver of time, Aware. It takes a long time to get to that moment, but when they do they are quite happy to die."

Then he began to weep his pretty puppet tears.

Félicité gave a very negative shake of the head. "But, dear one, it's all so indecent, so degrading, even for one of my Things."

He looked up in consternation, "Oh, Mother, I hope you don't think any of this is about sex. Sex is trivial, even when you don't know anything about it, and I assure you that I don't."

"My son, I know this much: you are not who you were. But who you are is not something that can be tolerated."

She looked almost menacing.

Percy saw his mother on the verge of a decision, a real decision with a very particular consequence for him. She was not just "saying." But wasn't this what he'd been waiting for? The end of saying things? The transcendent beginning of the Age of Acts? Irreconcilable Acts. He could do without the sex, but he really wasn't into the whole accepting-death thing, even though he was only technically alive. Still, there were a few more things that he needed to say.

She pulled the Sword of Finality out from her handbag.

"Forbearance, Mother, for just a moment. Let me tell you a story. Perhaps through it I can make myself understood. Then you can do what you like, reduce me to smutty cack, whatever, because there's nothing special about not existing, is there?"

22.

Jacques: When I cry, I often find I am stupid.
Master: And when you laugh?
Jacques: I find I am still stupid.

—DIDEROT, *JACQUES THE FATALIST*

—after Scheherazade

Oh, reader. She who has the last lack lacks best.

As you will recall, when we left the Queen of Spells and her prodigal golem, she had suspended the Sword of Finality over poor Percy's head. He was as insouciant as a puppet can be, and offered to tell a story before the fall of said sword. She must have agreed because here is the story.

"As you've surely surmised, dear Mother, there have been rough times for me since I left you, lo, these many months ago. I have been treated inhospitably by mothers, crudely by bleached-blond women in the morning, and cruelly by the constabulary. I have been sent into exile, and made to sleep in the grass with a dog family. All this before at last being given my own room in this house, and having my true calling given to me by tender Fanni.

"But my very lowest moment was while I was living with the dogs. That probably doesn't surprise you, but it sure surprised me. On the whole, the dogs were wonderful. Warm. Sympathetic. Helpful. Just a little smelly. I enjoyed my time with them, and I miss them now. Or, I miss most of them. There were a few 'head cases,' as they called it in that colorful—and really *loud*—language of theirs. These cases tended to be males with a sort of in-between status. They were not pups, who were nearly as clueless as I, and they were sure not the alpha, Alpha Benji, who set the rules for how this dog's life was to go. Nor were they among the small group of counselors called the Enforcers. No, it was the dogs that, if I were going to categorize them, I would call the Disappointed. The not-alphas and the not-Enforcers. They were the ones, as the scars on their brows testified, who had often been the *object* of enforcement. So, they were most often referred to by the dogs themselves as the Corrected.

"Let's face it, none of them liked being one of the Corrected, the one upon whom Alpha's wrath most often fell. Sure, inevitably, one day it would be from among the Corrected that the next alpha would come—it sure wouldn't come from the politically gelded Enforcers—but in the meantime this substantial group simmered in their resentment and their disappointment and their muscular sense of powerlessness. So, it's not surprising that now and then they 'let 'er rip,' as they said.

"And once, they let 'er rip on me. And why not? Who was I? A non-human human, a non-dog dog. That description was just too complicated, I was too complicated, Alpha's tolerance and kindness were too complicated. They liked simple things. A bouncing ball. A doggie Yum-Yum. A good firm bite to the hindquarters. These were the solid, substantial things of dog family life.

"Well, one morning I rose from among a heap of my furry companions, the chill morning rising in lazy plumes of steam off their warm bodies, and I headed across our little patch of trampled grass toward the place where a morning beverage was being prepared.

"Suddenly—for no reason at all, I'd made the short walk dozens of times before—one of the Corrected leaped from sleep and with a really angry bark sank his jaws into my calf. My leg went numb from the force of the bite, and I swung at him with my left hand. He let go of my leg in order to snatch at my hand that, fortunately, he was only able to graze.

"But then, my God, the uproar! All of my attacker's Corrected pals jumped up screaming 'Act out! Act out!' and came after me. I ran from the fold of my family as if I were a rude intruder.

"I'm told that the dogs gave a short chase and then returned to camp, tongues hanging from the sides of their heads in that happy way of theirs. I think for once in their lives they were a little proud of themselves. Unfortunately for them, they did not see what was coming. Alpha Benji was poised at the spear-end of a phalanx of Enforcers and a small army of the fiercest bitches. (And they could be quite fierce, the bitches.) Benji said, simply, 'He was one of ours.'

"They were incredulous. 'What? One of whose? That pasty-faced thing?'

"'Yeah, I got a good bite on his leg and that did not taste like no regular human leg. Tasted like the last time I got a slipper to chew on. What is that guy?'

"'Yeah, what the fuck? Good riddance.'

"But my Benji, bless him, was very Greek in such matters and very exacting in the laws of hospitality. Guests were not for running down, mauling, and eating. They had to be informed first that they were not guests, then let the mayhem begin, but I had not been so informed. However peculiar, I was in the pack.

"To make a long story short, the Corrected got their asses handed to them, once again, and they spent the rest of the day looking wistfully down on their erstwhile dog family from a distant hill."

Abruptly, there was a delicate knocking at the door. Fanni peeked in.

"Is everything all right in here, Percy? I thought I heard a dog bark."

The Queen of Spells turned and glared at her.

"No, darling girl, everything is fine," said Percy.

"He's not telling you any of those terrible stories about when he lived with the dogs, is he? They're a pack of lies." She grinned and squinched her face up at her little pun.

"Fanni, please, I'm talking to Mother."

The Queen calmed herself and asked, "There is more than one story?"

"Oh, my God, he's got a thousand and one of them. He'll talk your leg off. You'll be here all night. Speaking of which, do you have dinner plans, Mom? You're welcome to join us. Perhaps we could go out to the new farm-to-table restaurant for some grass-fed beef and whatever they happen to be doing with lentils and tiny carrots today. And of course the guest room is yours should you need it."

"No, thank you, I'll be leaving shortly."

"Too bad." She withdrew.

The Queen fixed Percy with a stare. "Now, are you done?"

"I'm sorry if the exposition was a little long. But it was full of action, don't you think? Rising action. Rising and howling action."

"Percy, I don't see the point of this. It seems desperate."

A voice from the next room.

"Percy!"

He groaned. "Sorry. *What?*"

"Can you come here?"

He looked at his grim mother. "No, I don't think so. What is it?"

"Are you going to be able to keep your three-thirty or not? Should I call Mrs., umm, what is that, Mrs. Yeasty?"

"That's fine, could you call her please?"

"Mrs. Yeasty?" asked the Queen.

"Yes. Some of them like to make up names," he explained to the Queen. "It's in part for just-in-case, but they also get a kick out of it. Sort of like they're undercover, I guess. This is at least the third name for Mrs. Yeasty. The odd thing is that she's a man."

"Honestly, I think this is quite enough. I think we need to make some decisions."

"No! You must let me tell this story! I am convinced that it will shed light on my situation."

Then Fanni appeared again at the door, holding a cellphone toward Percy.

"It's Mrs. Yeasty, Percy. He wants to talk to you. It seems urgent."

He took the phone from her, closed the door, and began to talk—and then he turned toward his mother and screamed!

23.

"We only want Tragedy if it can clench its side-muscles like hands on its belly, and bring to the surface a laugh like a bomb."

—WYNDHAM LEWIS, *BLAST #1*

"I'm sorry," said the Queen of Spells, "I lost my patience with you, and then my temper. I was impulsive. Does it hurt?"

"Well, you could simply have said, 'No, I don't want to hear any more stories,' instead of doing whatever it was you did to my arm. Is there a reason it just hangs there?"

"Sorry. I haven't used the Sword of Finality in a while. It requires a light touch when it is used for something less than Final."

"I admit, though, that whatever you did had an odd kind of compassion in it, because I don't feel any pain."

"I *am* sorry. I regret it now, but it doesn't make a lot of difference. I'll fix it when we get home."

"Will you let me go on with my story before we go?"

"Sure. I owe you that much."

"Okay, well, there I was then, bitten by my best friends, mauled even, bleeding, clothes torn, penniless, friendless, and isolated outside the walls of the city of humans. I staggered up a road that ran between walls of corn blocking my view in every direction. After some time, I came upon a man. I begged his help.

"He said, 'I can see that someone needs to help you, but if I help you I'll get blood all over my clothes. As you can see, I'm dressed for work, and it's a very nice suit. And I have no idea what your story is. Perhaps you have done something to bring this upon yourself. You could be a criminal.

"'I tell you what, if you'll just wait here, I'll run in to town and get more appropriate clothes. My gardening clothes. Oh, but, you know what? I have a ten o'clock meeting that I can't miss. Can this wait till my lunch break?'"

"Why didn't this man just call an ambulance on his cellphone?"

Percy stared at her in incomprehension.

"I'm sorry. It's my fault. You don't know about cellphones and such, and by tomorrow you'll have no need to know. But, I have heard that Americans are like this. Fearful and self-absorbed."

"Oh, Mother, they're not as bad as all that. They're just humans. Besides, it's not time to moralize yet. I'm just getting started."

"Okay. But this is a much better story than I expected."

"Thank you . . . "

Again, Fanni knocked at the door. This time it was a very loud, frustrated, impatient knock.

"Percy, it's Mrs. Yeasty, he called back . . . my God, what happened to your arm?" She gave Felicité a very suspicious look.

"It's okay, Fanni."

"But . . . "

"It's *okay*."

"Well, Mrs. Yeasty says that what he has to say cannot wait."

"Oh, all right. Give me the phone. Mrs. Yeasty? This is Percy . . . yes. Yes, I know. I am sorry about that. You're going to what? That's a very threatening thing to say, and a bad idea, but as far as my arms are concerned, you're too late. It's a long story. Mrs. Yeasty, if you persist in this kind of talk I'm afraid that the bony backtowards will no longer be available to you as a personal asset . . . I know . . . I know you're upset. Okay then. That's fine. Apology accepted. No, no, don't come over, I forgive you. Okay, I'm going to give the phone back to Fanni, and she'll take you through my calendar. Goodbye, Mrs. Yeasty. I love you too."

Percy rose, held up a finger as if to say "right back!", and went out.

Félicité waited a few minutes . . . but he *didn't* come back!

24.

"I shall be like a doctor tried by a jury of little boys on the accusation of a cook."

—SOCRATES IN PLATO'S *GORGIAS*

There are outtakes from the story of Percy's life, short scenes that were left on the cutting room floor, so to speak. These excised scenes still turn up now and then, in attics or buried in a library archive. It is the opinion of most critics that the cuts were made because the scenes were obscene; that is, they exceeded community standards for decency. Nothing wrong with that. Cut them, I say. His story maintains its narrative integrity in spite of all expurgation, so no harm done. At last count, two hundred and twenty-seven scenes have been found. This group of outtakes is often referred to by cognoscenti as "Non-canonical Mayhem," or, informally, the Mayhem Years.

Some of these excised scenes were taken out because they were too silly. Given the silliness of what was left in, I can't quite understand how anything was ever found to be *too* silly.

Consider this:

LOST SCENE A 12358.1, "LACKING CHARACTER" (COPYRIGHT ABSOLUTE OPTICS AND TRANSLATENT CRANIALS, LLC).

One day the Alpha dog, Benji, took pity on Percy and said, "You know, you don't have to sleep out here with us. I know the townies said they had moral and legal cause for casting you out, but if you had some money they'd let you back in, trust me."

"I don't have any money."

"True. But you're human, so you can get some."

"How?"

"Most of the humans who have had to spend some time out here with us usually say something like, 'I've had it out here with you guys. No offense, but I've had it. I'm going to rob a convenience store.'"

"And that works?"

"Well, we have never seen one of them again, so we think it must work."

"Okay, I'm willing to give it a try. What's a convenience store?"

Benji rolled his dog eyes and said, "It's a kind of store. They sell doughnuts. Let's leave it at that for now."

"'Kay."

"One other thing is you'll need a gun. They always take a gun."

"I don't have a gun."

"Not a problem. Here, take this."

It was two short chicken bones tied together with twine in the shape of a gun.

Percy took the gun, stuck it in his pants at the small of his back, and walked back through the city gate. He soon found a Country Panic convenience store. It was about 11 p.m. and there appeared to be only one employee inside, so Percy went in, walked up to the register, and said, "Give me money, please."

The clerk's eyes popped open, but his face expressed not fear but amazement.

"Oh, shit! Are you serious?"

"I sure am."

"Listen, you can't rob me tonight. Come on! This is my *first* night working here. The very first one. How would you feel?"

"So, this *is* a robbing. I'm doing it right?"

"What?"

"I don't see what difference it makes if I rob you tonight or come back tomorrow."

"Besides, you don't even have a gun."

"Yes, I do." He pulled the chicken-bone gun from the back of his pants.

"That's your gun? Where did you get that? Did a dog give it to you?"

"Yes, as a matter of fact, a dog did give it to me. How did you know?"

"Because that's a dog-gun, man. It's not a real gun. Let me see that thing."

Handing the gun over, Percy said, "Then why did they give it to me?"

"Because they're dogs! They're stupid! They think these things are real guns, but they're not."

"This is really confusing, but I'm still robbing you. I need money so I can stop sleeping with the dogs."

"Are you listening to me? I told you. This is my first night, so you can't rob me. Why don't you just shoplift some things and call it good."

"I need money."

"Don't press your luck! You can get money another time when you've got a real gun."

"All right."

The clerk handed him a bag and he started putting Jelly Bellies, beef jerky, Ho Ho's, and whatever else was close by in the bag. As he began to walk out, the clerk signaled him over, took the bag, and started going through it. At just that moment, a man pulled up in a pickup truck and came in. He was a typical midwestern haystack with a dirty Cargill Seed cap on.

"Hey," he said to the clerk.

"Hey."

"What's goin' on?"

"This guy tried to rob me with this dog-gun. I confiscated it."

He showed it to the man. "A dog-gun! My kids love these things. I have a little collection of them." Looks it over. "Hey, this is a really good one. Look at the quality of the twine wrap. First rate. You could almost believe it was a real gun if . . . "

The two looked at Percy and in unison said, "If you were a dog!"

They laughed.

"Well, I can't fuck around with you two all night. I just need to turn in a propane canister and get a new one."

"Here's the key to the case. Just take one, and bring the key back. I've got to keep an eye on this character."

Mr. Haystack took the key, went out, and a minute later they heard his truck tires squeal as he took off.

"Son of a bitch!"

The clerk ran out, then returned quickly.

"He stole two tanks and he even took the damned key! Might as well kiss this job goodbye."

While all this was going on, Percy was putting his shoplifted items back in the bag.

"Whoa!" said the clerk. "I've had it. I've fucking had it. Let me see what you've got there. A twelve-count case of *Nature's Harvest Organic Natural Wholesome Grain Nutrition Bars Without Seeds, Sticks, or Stems*? I don't think so. That's like twenty bucks. Come on. I try to give you a break and you pull this."

"What should I take, then?" Percy was crying now. Just a little bit, but he was crying.

The clerk frowned in disgust, threw a package of Ding Dongs at him, and said, "Now get your sorry ass out of here. I'm calling the cops."

25.

"You're not really supposed to understand me, but I want very much for you to listen to me."

—SCHLEGEL

Among the many outtakes—whether obscene, silly, or stupefying—there is a dialogue between Percy and the Queen of Spells as they sat in Fanni's house. I'm going to leave while you read it because, frankly, it's embarrassing. It's transcendentally silly or just silly as shit, depending on your philosophical orientation.

"Mother, there is one thing that has been bothering me since I found a home here with Fanni. It's something that I think you can best explain."

"I'll try."

"Well, many of my clients have been disappointed in my cock."

"Percy! Do you need to talk like that?"

"That's what they call it here, if you know what I'm referring to, and I don't know why you would. Before I came here, I didn't call it anything. I'm not even sure that I'd noticed it."

She frowned.

"Yes, I know what it is. I must say that I'm disappointed that you do."

"What's the big deal?" He paused with a startled look on his face. "Did you just feel something? A sort of shaking?"

"Never mind that. What is your question?"

"Well, the source of their disappointment has something to do with its size. They say it's smallish. Actually, it's been the occasion for some really deep philosophical conversations about the relative merits of . . . there it is again!"

"What?"

"The shaking."

"I didn't feel a thing."

"Wow. Okay, the merits of how I was made. The idea is that if I am a being that was made through an act of Will, your Will, and as an expression of freedom on your part, then it is not strictly logical to say that I have a smallish cock."

"Could you please say 'penis.' I am your mother, after all. Oh! Now I felt it! Is it an earthquake?"

"In Illinois?" He waits to see if it will happen again. Nothing. "Anyway, there are times when a child must say to his progenitor, 'Look things in the face!' This is one of those times."

"I am trying, Percy, believe me."

"Okay, then please forbear. So, it is not strictly logical to say I have a smallish penis because it is not even clear that the penis is mine since the Will that made the penis is not mine but yours. Do you understand?"

"I think so."

"Anyway, Fanni has often said that if I ever had the chance I ought to ask you about it. So, here are the options you had at the moment of my creation, as well as I can understand them."

Now a rapid series of booms, and our interlocutors reach out to each other and steady themselves against the table.

"Goodness!" said the Queen.

"I think it's done. I hope it's done. Anyway, your options: first, and most obvious, you could've given me a larger penis. From what I've heard, that is the option that most of my clients would have preferred, imagining that they'd had some say in the matter. They say things like, 'It would be nice to see you with a real wad.'"

"Oh, my child!"

"The second option is the one you chose, a very standard-sized, or maybe standard-sized-minus penis. Third, you could have given me a tiny penis, but that would have been cruel, and you are not cruel, so we'll dismiss that one. Finally, intriguingly, you had the option of giving me no penis at all. You could have made that area as smoothed over as the crotch of a crash test dummy, which is in most ways what I am."

"That's not true. It hurts me to hear you say that. You're a very special boy!"

"Out of curiosity, could you just go through your decision-making process?"

"I'd rather not."

"Come on! You're making me, you're filling in the blanks, this kind of hand, this kind of nose, and you come to that region and you say . . . what?"

"My child, there is no answer to the question you're really asking. Frankly, the answer to the question you think you're asking is easy: I didn't give it much thought. You got the standard, default penis that I give my male creatures when I make them. But the question you're really asking is not 'Why did you make my penis medium-sized?' but 'Why did you make me at all?' What grieves me is that not even that gets at it. You're not asking a question, you're making a statement: 'I wish you hadn't made me.' It's very painful for me to say, but you've convinced me that you are right, I never should have made you. It wasn't fair to you, whatever that means. I should have stuck with the little clones on horseback. They serve their purpose, deliver their messages, then they're done, gone, up in greasy smoke like a bucket of chicken wings tossed in a fire pit. Or I can give them to my grandchildren as stocking stuffers at Christmas."

Percy got a sudden look of enlightenment on his face and said, "You're right. Those are my thoughts, though I never thought them. Thank you."

So saying, he raised to his face again his black Zorro mask. Then, from behind the mask, emerging as if from the prophetic catacombs of Thebes, came his voice, transformed, saying, "But what you do not understand, dear Queen Mother, is that I am no longer your shiny creature to make or unmake. I have stepped into the path of fate, and I am the overseer of the inner life of the little people of N—. They come to me and I lead them either to self-understanding or to the eccentric sphere of the dead. In either case, it is a good thing that I provide, because at least now there is no uncertainty regarding their destinies.

"Still, just like you, I have wondered about whether what I do is good. Whether *I* am good. So I asked God."

The Queen raised her arm as if it were God's true instrument, his thunderbolt. "Blasphemy!"

"Don't get all upset! I described for Him what I did, in simple terms, omitting nothing, and all He did was laugh. Do you know why He laughed? He laughed because God enjoys a good joke. Because in the end if God can't laugh, who can laugh? So, laugh, Mother!"

Apparently the Queen Mother wasn't in the mood for laughter because that is the end of the discarded scene. Personally, I'd like to think that she did laugh. Talking to God! Come on!

In any case, it's interesting to see that even puppets can have their little *anagnorises*. And, in the end, admit it, who *isn't* a puppet? Who isn't in a play? It's enough to give one hope.

I can, however, tell you this, for what it's worth: I suspect that while Felicité and her Thing were talking, directly below their feet, sedimentary rock was compressed from the side through a shrinking of the crust of the Earth. The effect of this compression was that layers of rock were thrown suddenly into folds, sending waves of energy through the rock. This explains the "shaking" they reported.

Now, this was all Nature's doing and none of my own. The problem is that by intruding in this way Nature threatened the scene with a rigid and lifeless academicism. Nature puts the inner vitality of the scene in jeopardy with a fusty old theatrical device: an earthquake. Another fucking *deus ex machina*. What next? Flashing lights and the shaking of foil in the wings? No wonder this scene found its way to the cutting room floor.

I would not bring this up if it were just this one instance. Unhappily, as the history of art has shown time and again, Nature makes a habit of ruining the artist's best effort in just this way. Which leads me to wonder, is it your impression that Nature itself is merely an example of the imitative fallacy? *

26.

"With us, the tender, imaginative power of mothers appears to express itself only in monsters."

—LESSING

There have been some changes. As you will recall, Percy left the room to take a phone call from Mrs. Yeasty and didn't return. In dog vernacular, he ran away. Well, he was soon enough dragged back to Fanni's by the Queen of Spells. She knew that he wasn't intending to come back on his own. She suspected that he would try to hide down the street at Gerald's, and that's where he was, in the backyard, curled up in a large concrete culvert for storm water. Gerald offered no physical objections to the Queen because he understood the need for discipline, especially a mother's. In fact, he claimed that he himself had been naughty recently and wondered if she had the time to discipline him or at least tell him how she might discipline him if she had the time. She rewarded him with a *look*. You can imagine this murderous look, which is a good thing because I can't do it justice.

---

* There is one other possibility. After I left the room to allow the reader to experience the scene's full silliness, I passed the time hitting tennis balls against the wall in the next room. Perhaps that was it, and not an earthquake. If so, my apologies.

As for Gerald, speaking of this "look," he said, "Oooooh, that's right, isn't it? Pretty, very *pretty*."

Unfortunately, once found, Percy thrashed around some, a little fish on a big hook, did some very special pleading and so forth, and Felicité was forced to take frankly damaging counter-measures.

At any rate, there he sat again, across from her, back at Fanni's. His left arm dangled lifelessly at his side (but you knew about that), his right eye was swollen shut. Most alarmingly, his jaw was unhinged. To tell you the truth, he looked a little like one of those Middle Eastern tyrants after they've been caught and treated to some rough justice by the peasantry. Stranger still, behind him was good Fanni, hanging in the air in mid-leap, like that Air Jordan silhouette, only she's got a baseball bat, not a basketball. The Queen of Spells was apparently forced to put the air-fix on her, so there she hung, witless and butterflied.

The Queen had made herself some herbal tea, and she sat quietly while Percy considered the wreckage.

At last, she said, "Now, Percy, what was all that about?"

"I'm shorry. I panked." He didn't speak well, what with the flapping jaw.

"And you were so convincingly stoic just minutes before. Even though I didn't like what you were saying, I was impressed."

"I tink da shayink is: I losht my nooiv."

"You sound like the mayor of Chicago!" She looked at him thoughtfully, then smiled. "And you know, with a few more pranks like that you might just become a real boy yet."

" . . . "

"It hurts, doesn't it?"

"No, of coursh nop. I'm nop weal."

She mocked him. "Oh, would you like to feel the pain, too?"

"Don'p tumble youshelf."

"So, are we done, then?"

He looked up at her imploringly. "I gnow I don'p desherve it, but do you fink I coo finish my shtory?"

Another indulgent smile. The Queen knew how all of this had to end, but what difference would another few minutes make?

"Sure, Percy. Proceed. But first let me fix your jaw. It's all smashed over by your ear and you're not speaking very clearly. I probably didn't need to thrash you quite that hard, but I was trying to make a point. There."

"Thanks."

"You're welcome." Seeing him whole again, she recalled just how fond she had once been of her Thing.

"Well, where was I? I was on a country road looking nearly as bloody and abused as I do now."

A queenly scowl.

"I met a man who thinks he should help, but he also has reservations. He has just said something about waiting till his lunch break, to which I replied, 'No, that won't help. I won't have a drop of ichor in my body by then.'

"The man looked puzzled when I said that. 'Ichor?' he asked.

"'Mmmm, hydraulic fluid?'

"'You have hydraulic fluid?'

"'It doesn't make much difference, so let's call it blood. It is reddish. Or would you say magenta?'

"'Look, I don't care. The only thing I have to say is that I can see my way clear to helping you here if you can compensate me for my time. After all, I may miss an opportunity for profit if I'm late for my meeting.'

"'You mean money, don't you?'

"'Are you from another planet? Of course I mean money.'

"'It so happens that I don't have any. That's part of my problem. If I had money I wouldn't be out here bleeding to death on this country road.'

"'Nothing? No checking, savings, bonds, or credit? No family or friends to hit up?'

"'Nothing.'

"'Have you tried knocking off a convenience store?'

"I sighed. 'I've tried that, but I'm not good at it.'

"'Well, hell, no one's good at it the first time.'

"He sat down and studied me.

"At last he said, 'Look, I gotta go. But I wanna wish you the very best.'"

Percy stopped. Suddenly, he looked old, tired, and discouraged.

"Is that it?" asked the Queen. "Did he really leave you bleeding on the road? And by the way, I don't know where you dreamed up this ichor/hydraulic fluid thing. That is honest-to-God real blood I gave you. It is red and it carries oxygen. There's some of it drying on your chin if you want proof."

Percy smiled a forlorn smile. "I'm nearly done. So, just as the man was about to walk away, he gave me a kick that sent me down an embankment. He came over, looked down at me, and said, 'In case you don't die down there, remember, this conversation never happened. Anyway, I am what we call "leaving you for dead." That's not something I ever thought I'd actually do, but for some reason it doesn't feel all that unfamiliar. It feels like something I've *intended* a million times before. It's always been there, hasn't it? In me. Waiting for its chance. Huh! What do you know! This little encounter has been very enlightening. Thanks for that!'"

Percy looked up at the Queen, a sad puppy. He looked as if he really had been kicked down into some ditch to die.

"Well, go on."

"I'm done."

"That's your story?"

"I know it's anticlimactic, but I give up."

"So, is there a moral to your story?"

"Are you kidding? What do I know about morals? I can only tell this story at all because Benji, Alpha storyteller as well as Alpha, liked to tell it while sitting around a fire at night. His ending was always, 'And then wild dogs came and ate him!' No preparation, no plausibility, no effort to explain. It was just how they wanted the story to end, so it did. Dogs come and eat everybody.

"And, oh, how they howled! That was the whole point of the story, not some moral. They got to imagine being wild beasts and eating humans. That really rocked their little world. It was like dog porn. Some of the Enforcers would always get carried away and start banging at the bitches, making Benji smile in amusement. Me? I'd sneak away from the fire before they got to that part, because it was scary."

"So none of that happened to you?"

"Of course not. I was just trying to make you feel sorry for me. I was buying time, and it's the only story I know."

"Percy, I know you're upset. I know you may even feel a little desperate just now. But did you *really* live with dogs?"

"Yes, of course."

"And they talked to you and told stories?"

"Sure they did."

"*Percy* . . ."

"What?"

Felicité was more convinced than ever that there was something defective in her Thing.

"All I was hoping was that I could tell a story that would persuade you not to do what you're going to do. That's really all I was thinking, but I give up. Whether I tell a good story or a bad, it doesn't matter. I will never prove to you that I am not what I think you think I am."

The Queen of Spells looked long at her creature. Her eyes began to tear up. "Oh, Percy! That's very sad and sweet! In spite of it all, I am fond of you!"

She stood to her full majestic height, like Athena towering over the fields of Troy. She reached both hands toward him, and . . . gently rolled him up inside a glass ball.

As she walked out of the room, smiling and peering into the ball as if it were a Christmas snow globe, with her trailing hand she released Fanni from her spell with a graceful flip of her wrist, and the poor woman fell to the floor, banging her chin and knees with an audible "Oof!" and "Ouch!"

Outside, the day was clear and the afternoon light was splendid. It illuminated Percy prettily. Any child would have been delighted to put him high up in a Christmas tree. You may think I'm making this up, but as Felicité walked away, Percy dangling in cheerful sparkles from her hand, I saw his eye, round like the globe he was sunk in, brightly *wink*.

27.

"When a man is told 'You are this kind of person because your skull-bone is constituted in such and such a way,' this means nothing else than, 'I regard a bone as your reality.'"

—HEGEL

Among the outtakes I earlier provided for you, there is one very, very different (if not contradictory) version of the story of Percy's suffering on the road after having been mauled by the family dogs. Actually, it's not entirely clear that it is Percy's story. There are now many who believe that it is actually another of the *dog* stories. In short, Percy may have been telling the Queen the truth about dog narratives—like us, dogs enjoy a good yarn. And, hold on to your hat, the possibility that this version was told first by a dog or dogs has the ethnographic anthropology community buzzing about an imminent paradigm shift in their field.

It is not the crude sensationalism of talking dogs that excites scholars, nor is it the celebrity that captured a few of them after the glamorous articles in the Style section of *The New York Times*. Rather, they claim, it is the moral complexity and spiritual insight of the story itself that excites them, especially in the way that the moral complexity is colored by the idea that it is a dog that is telling the story.

One of these scholars, in private conversation with me, called this story a "game changer in our understanding of dog narratives." While he spoke to me off the record and I will respect that commitment, I can fairly observe that he had a dubious backstory of his own. While doing research ("thick description") in the open woodlands of southern Africa with a pack of *lycaon pictus*, the distinguished professor's descriptions got a little too thick and he went native. This is not unusual among ethnographic anthropologists, but the present case went some way beyond what is common. Upon his return to the United States, the scholar in question greeted his student interns—both male and female—by sniffing their genitals. For those of his colleagues who came of age in the campus atmosphere of the '60s and '70s, this behavior was not unfamiliar, but for his PC colleagues of the present it was crucifixion time. In any event, I think you can see why this case, as told by Percy's dog companions, was so important to him: he hoped to rehabilitate his reputation in this very small community of scholars.

For the moment, I think it's best for me simply to pass this whatever-it-is, game changing evidence or insanity, along without further comment. (I have deleted the vague growling sounds and the occasional barking uttered by the canine "native informant" from the text as it appeared originally in *Chats Partout: an Ethnographic Journal of Animal Cultures*. I have never claimed to be a scholar, and so I do not feel bound by their rigorous professional ethics. For me, it was best to leave the translation of barking to the pros.) For what it's worth, here it is.

After the business executive had kicked Percy into the culvert and gone off to make his 10 o'clock appointment, Percy dragged himself back up to the road. Sitting there, he came to Sudden Enlightenment; that is, he found himself unexpectedly Awake. In a moment, he had come to understand that all this business about being a real person was an illusion. So he resolved to give himself away.

Late in the morning, traffic picked up on the road. Residents came and went, among them farmers, merchants, and many ordinary people, colorfully clad, on bicycles and in cars. As they passed, Percy's mind was electric with his happiness. So he shouted out, "Who wants a man? Free man here! First come, first served!"

Most of the passersby didn't even notice him. The cyclists yelled, "On your left!" and moved on, attention fixed on their power meters. Others whizzed by in their cars because they had their own profitable appointments to keep. A few who did notice his condition merely scowled and threw pocket change in his direction. After many hours of persistently shouting out his strange offer, a man stopped. He looked into Percy's face and asked, "Are you serious?"

"Yes, I am."

"You're not just a day laborer, are you? You don't just want to cut my lawn?"

"No, no. I'm giving myself away, for what that's worth. I'm not real, you know. I'm just a soap bubble on the face of time. I'm the dream in a dreamer's dream."

He looked at Percy, all beaten and torn, yet still coming on with this mixed metaphor and teenage existentialism, and smirked.

"You know, actually, I could use a man. I make homeopathic medicines and I've been wanting to make this salve, but it requires human bone marrow. I've offered to buy some from people who have just lost family members, but they've all been scandalized by the suggestion. It's frustrating. I have a great concept and a great website but no product. I'm a startup, but I have no capital. And until I have a product that I can put in a bottle, and until I have somebody else's money for production, how am I supposed to have an IPO? And without an IPO, how am I supposed to sell the company and retire as a young billionaire?"

Percy bounced up and down with happiness. "If you want me, I am yours to do with as you like!"

"For free?"

"Absolutely free."

"Well, there is the little problem that you're not dead; you're alive, and therefore your marrow is being used at the moment."

"Oh, I'm dead all right."

"You are fucking with me, aren't you? I don't usually allow people to fuck with me. I should kill you for that alone, then take your marrow."

"That works for me. But if it helps I'll say that I never existed at all."

After this odd pronouncement, the man was more dubious than ever.

"Excuse me, but that don't make a lot of sense."

"Well, let me show you then. You don't happen to have a knife, do you?"

"Better yet, I have a hacksaw that I take with me wherever I go, just in case."

"Okay, then, let's go! Give me the saw!"

They started in on a thigh, but, unfortunately, the saw was rusty and dull, so they had to take turns hacking at his leg. By the time they were done, they were perspiring and exhausted.

"Whew!" said the man. "I'm all done in. For a guy who doesn't really exist, you sure are hard."

Percy was lying back, panting. "Sorry, I had no idea."

"Well, let's see what we got."

He lifted the stump of Percy's leg and peered in.

"What the hell is this?"

"What is it?"

"I can't use this shit! I have to look after product quality, you know. Christ. All that work for nothing, plus I'm late now."

"Well, could you tell me what you see in there?"

The man leaned over and closed one eye.

"It's hard to see."

He took out a lighter and flipped it on. He looked again. A fatty flap of tissue caught fire.

"Well, I'll be damned."

"What is it?"

"It's spongy, or cheesy—a whey product? Greek yoghurt is not out of the question. Or tile grout? I feel that I could caulk a bathtub with it, or make a spread for canapés. There are almost-microscopic threads, reddish, suggesting a use in woven high-tech fabrics. I'm also tempted to say Cheez Whiz, but I don't want to offend you."

"Cheez Whiz is bad?"

"Some places—the bone, I suppose—are grainy like fine pumice. It flakes, and I can imagine someone saying that it's desiccated. A very compelling contrast to the Whiz. If you were a work of art, I could comment on the dramatic juxtaposition of textures."

He looked at Percy quizzically.

"You're not a work of art, are you?"

Replying frankly, Percy said, "I don't think so. But perhaps that depends on whatever juxtaposition means."

"Look, sorry to have put you through all this, but you're just not at all what I had in mind for my product line."

As suddenly as he had achieved inner clarity, Percy was struck with the stupidity of what he had done. Enlightened? He was worthless, not human, not someone's Thing, not even a work of art. Plus he now only had one leg and would have to hop just to get back down in the ditch, if he could get up at all. Perhaps this inventor of New Age salves would help by giving him a good kick and rolling him down, like the businessman had done earlier.

"I'm sorry too," he said, "I feel like I've failed you."

Our homeopath entrepreneur looked puzzled and sad. Disappointed. Then, suddenly, *he* was enlightened! He saw the futility of trying, of grasping at worldly things, even the idea of seeing his salve on the shelves at Whole Foods no longer excited him. And he saw Percy now not as raw material but as part of a world of creatures that was suffering, in part because of his own folly, and he felt great compassion for him.

"Listen," he said, "I feel like *I* have disappointed *you*. I offered you hope but I failed."

Tiny high-viscosity tears gathered in Percy's eyes and rolled down like leaking brake fluid.

The man was abashed. He said, "Hey, let me help you get this leg back on your stump. I have some duct tape in the car and I'll drive you to an emergency room or to a body shop, whatever you need. They can perform miracles with carbon fiber."

"No thanks."

"It's no trouble."

"Forget it. I think I'd just like to be alone."

Not knowing what else to do, he placed the leg in Percy's lap where it sat like an alien appendage.

"Well, see ya."

"See ya."

Just then they heard a howling and yelping in the near distance, growing ever closer.

And they were afraid.

Story done, Alpha-Benji-Dog-God assumed a *Samadhi* pose and breathed slowly, the air passing rhythmically in and out through the gate of his lungs, his black lips pouting and quietly salivating.

28.

"Sending the young out into life with such a false psychological orientation is as if one were to equip people going on a polar expedition with summer clothing and maps of the Italian lakes."

—FREUD

—after Diderot

Eventually, the Marquis sat Jake in the last chair at the last rickety table in the château and said, "Jake, I've reached a shocking and sad conclusion. We are no longer grand. We could call ourselves the *nouveau pauvre*, and I grant you that would have some remnant dignity in it, but even then we'd be kidding ourselves. We are like the aged *grande dame* in her rotting mansion who greets the doctor from the poor farm in her queenly silk shawl—never mind the gaps where moths and worms have eaten through and even begun to munch on her! In other words, we are *done*."

This was not news to Jake. "I know, Grandpa, we are poor," he said.

"Poor! There'd be some hope in mere poverty. We are rotting gods! And there is worse news. According to my banker, if we don't acquire something called an income stream, we won't even have this little château of ours. Then will come the last indignity: camping with those Occupy the Marquis people and living off donated sandwiches. I will be occupying myself! And I'm just about mad as hell enough to do it! And when that ends, we'll simply be among the homeless, although even that term puts gold brocade on the corpse."

Self-pitying tears gathered in his eyes.

He continued, "And then who will protect us from the aliens?!

No one! They will run roughshod! And we, helpless, victims to every cruel alien whim! Oh, there will be a price to pay for my earlier excesses. But this will not go easy for these bankers, I promise you that. With the last of my resources I am building a turret on the roof, and I will place a forty-four-caliber machine gun in it. I got one on eBay yesterday. It says some assembly is required. I don't suppose you've ever put one of these together, have you?"

Jake looked to see if his grandpa were kidding about all this. He didn't seem to be, and that worried him. He was under a lot of stress. Was he breaking down? Hallucinating? Was this the onset of dementia? Or was their earlier glory the hallucination?

"Grandpa, to tell you the truth, I don't think it would be so bad, living in a tent, even with Occupy people. It might even be fun to occupy Occupy. Actually, I was sitting with them just yesterday talking about music and philosophy and equality. I liked them."

A reasonably horrified look from the Marquis.

"And just think how simple everything would be. No wife for me, no Rory for you."

"Jake, do not, *do not*, go all mendicant on me. Not now. Not in our moment of crisis. Trust me, a tent is not a good thing. We need to be thinking seriously about what to do, not indulging in Boy Scout fantasies. So let's put our heads together over this income-stream thing."

"Well, what do you think the bankers mean by it?"

The Marquis rose up and looked into Jake's eyes. "It means you have to find a job."

"Find a job? Why me?"

"*You* because you are the next generation, our future, in which we place great trust. *Find* because, apparently, they are hidden. The jobs, I mean."

"I wouldn't know anything about it."

"I know, I know, and I blame myself for that."

Now, of course, Jake could have said, "Why don't *you* find a job? It's *your* château." But he didn't. You know Jake, by now. He had never done anything more than pay for Fanni's dinner and hunch over Xbox controls, but that was not his fault. He'd never been given anything more to do. But, to his credit, he also didn't put on airs. How could he? There was no room for air, thanks to Fanni's firebombing of his heart.

"I don't know, Grandpa. I don't think I can do it."

"Oh, my boy, cheer up. You'll figure it out. Now, here's what I'd like you to do. I'd like you to leave and seek a job. Call it a quest. A young man needs a good quest. Very romantic. And I'll send Rory along to keep you company. I think I can spare him for a few years."

The Marquis laughed. The idea of life without Rory was a happy idea, especially if it didn't involve moving into a tent.

Jake stared at the Marquis, mouth wide.

"Well, if you don't like quests, let's start by thinking of it as a vacation then, how about that? Surely you can handle that. But what is a vacation a vacation from? A job! So what I'm thinking is this: start with the vacation and that will develop naturally into a vacation companion piece: a job! And thus: an income stream!"

"This is very confusing, Grandpa."

"A stream, my boy, a mountain stream! What a lovely word! And what a wonderful world! A world in which things are the way they are because that's the way they are! That's the kind of clear thinking we need! And you're just the right kind of boy for it: a working boy! It is time to serve! You are called to duty! Rise up now and shine! Make me proud of you! Serve your country, or at least serve me!"

The very next morning Jake and Rory set out on their job search. True, Jake did it with some reluctance and for two very particular reasons. First, he had no idea of what he was doing, what he was looking for, or how he would know if he found it. Second, he was half convinced that his grandfather was, as someone somewhere used to say, "tetched." But, as we know, Jake was a sensitive boy and he always tried to do what he was told.

The truth is that Jake and Rory set out on beat-up bicycles that had been left behind by the Occupy the Marquis people, but that sounds pathetic. So, at the risk of an anachronism, I'd like to propose that we say they were on horses. Nice horses, well brushed, shiny, and with big brown eyes that were intelligent if always just a little frightened.* Everyone loves a beautiful horse, whereas if I said that they were on bicycles so beat-up that not even the bottom 1% of the bottom 99% would bother with them, you'd lose all respect for their journey. So, let's go with the horses.

So Jake and Rory were going up old Route 51 on their horses when Jake said to Rory, "Do you know what a job is?"

"Well, sir, to the best of my knowledge there are two kinds of job. The first is a greeter. The second hands over the French fries."

"That's it?"

"That seems to be the consensus of opinion. It's true that there are some, called *geeks*, who have jobs working with computers, but that is not for us. They are our betters, as the Marquis might say." He sighed. "The sad thing is that he continues to believe he is a superior being, a member of the nobility. Of course, there is no nobility, and, as well you know, he has no

---

* Why is it that horses always look terrified? You know, on edge so that a little mouse could send them running in horror across the countryside, your eight-year-old son hanging on for dear life? I always want to say to them, "Look, you have nothing to fear, you're *big*!"

life outside what has been provided for him by those very geeks, hence his precious *Halo*."

"What about your job?"

"Precisely."

"Do you mean that you are a greeter?"

"I have greeted people. Sometime, I'd love to tell you about the night I greeted the masked man."

"A masked man?"

"Yes. He was a faggot."

" . . . ?"

"A pile driver?"

" . . . ?"

"Let's leave that for now."

"I just want to understand what you're saying."

"Well, then, I think it's most accurate to say that my job with the Marquis has transcended its origins."

"I think it means you don't do anything at all, and you are exploiting my papa's kindness."

"Or his stupidity."

Jake gave Rory a hard look.

Rory, brightly: "But come, sir, we'll have lots of time to talk about jobs. Why don't we talk about sex instead? Isn't that what men do when they travel beyond the hearing of women?"

Jake groaned. "You sound like my wife."

Coyly, "Sir!"

"Sex is what I'm trying to leave behind. I don't understand why people get so excited about it. It seems trivial to me. I think that if someone just stood up and said that once, we'd all come to our senses. Someone, some innocent, needs to point at it in its ridiculousness and say, 'Why are they doing that silly thing?' and it would all just come tumbling down, the whole corrupt edifice."

Rory looked at Jake skeptically. "That sounds anti-American, sir."

"Look, we have a long way to go, so why don't we just ride in silence for a while?"

"Hmmm. Silence is not my strong suit. Would you mind if I dropped back a few yards and talked to myself?"

They rode north in silence for the remainder of the day, although every now and then Rory could be heard giggling, like a little parrot that is happy with itself.

29.

"Modern man drags along with him a huge quantity of indigestible stones."

—NIETZSCHE

It wasn't just that Rory bugged him. It was more the depressing feeling that bringing Rory along meant bringing along the world he was trying to leave behind: a world of confusion and pain.

This raw fact was brought home for Jake on the first night. They were setting up Jake's little pup tent on the side of the road. Rory had a small duffel bag full of all sorts of things none of which was a tent. He spread them out on the ground in front of Jake's tent.

Of particular note, the duffel contained: a fragment of a map, a sealed letter without an address, a lottery ticket, and a revolver, a Smith and Wesson snub-nose .38, a cop gun or a midnight special, depending on which direction it is facing.

"Why did you bring this stuff?"

Rory wagged his head like a Hindu: "I brought only what was essential."

"Essential? Essential to what?"

"Sir, our quest! Our saga! Our legend! Our little drop of water in the Ocean of Story!"

"I know I'm going to be sorry for asking, but what are you talking about?"

"Isn't it obvious? The map is in case we get lost."

"But you can't even see what it's a map of."

"Well, if you're going to be difficult, then it's a map showing us our destination. See the big X there? It marks the spot. So, when we find the whole map that this is part of, we will be able to go to the place I've marked."

"You marked it?"

"Yes."

"And I suppose you also tore this piece from the map."

Rory glowed.

"Then you should know where we're going."

This time, a glorious smile.

"Well, don't tell me. I don't want to ruin the surprise. What about the letter?"

"Interesting point, sir. At present, we do not know whom it is for. But when we get to the place on the map, we will know, and we will address it to her."

"How do you know it's a woman?"

"Sir, unlike the masked man, I am not a cowboy swish."

" . . . "

"A *maricón*? Do you speak Spanish?"

"And the lottery ticket?"

"That, sir, is a winning ticket and the end of all our worries about jobs. But you should note that it is only half of the ticket."

"And so we're also looking for the person who has the other half?"

"Yes."

"So we're looking for a map, the address for the intended recipient of a sealed letter, and the owner of the other half of a lottery ticket. That's a lot of looking."

"I thought it would cheer you up and keep you busy in case the job hunt was discouraging."

Jake looked thoughtfully at Rory's possessions, which were laid out so neatly before his little tent. He smiled.

"Has it occurred to you that the other half of the lottery ticket might be in the envelope?"

Rory laughed disdainfully. "Oh, sir, that is a wicked thought. Nevertheless, that may very well be true. But the letter also contains a curse. It can only be opened by the person to whom it is addressed."

"A curse?"

"A curse."

"And who cursed it? You?"

"Sir!"

"But we won't know who the letter is addressed to until we get to the spot on the map."

"Correct."

"At which point we mail the letter."

"Right."

"But then we have to go seeking the woman to whom it is addressed, in order to get the other half of the ticket?"

"Very good, sir."

"Why don't we just take the letter with us and hand it to her?"

"That is a devious thought. It's no wonder your life has come to such ruin that you must seek a job."

"Never mind that. Okay, so let's say I play along. We mail the envelope and follow it ourselves. But she won't be at that address, will she?"

"Probably not."

"But there's something else there, right?"

"There may be a sealed box there that grants wishes so long as you don't open the box."

"I have a few wishes."

"That's only human, sir."

"Is there ever an end to our saga?"

"That's not for me to say."

"Okay, I get it. So, let's say, purely speculatively, that in desperate, drunken despair I open the envelope now."

"Oh, my dear boy, that is what the handgun is for."

Later:

Jake: "I can't believe you didn't bring a sleeping bag."

"Cuddles?"

Later.

"Rory?"

"Mmm-hmmm?"

"Did I understand you correctly? If I open the letter, you will shoot me?"

Laughing. "Yes, obviously, but that shouldn't worry you because you would never . . . sir! What are you thinking?"

"Nothing, Rory. Go to sleep. Are you warm now?"

30.

Complacencies of the peignoir, and late
Coffee and oranges in a sunny chair,
And the green freedom of a cockatoo . . .

—WALLACE STEVENS

—after Flann O'Brien

—I thought cockatoos were white.

—They are.

—But this one is lemon yellow.

—And that one's orange orange.

She laughed obscurely.

—Can I assume that this is not a real cockatoo but one of your made-up things?

—Please, you'll hurt his feelings! Actually, he's quite a bit better than a real cockatoo because he can recite poetry. But you should be careful about what you request. If you ask for *Paradise Lost*, you'd better get some coffee, because you'll get it, all night and into the next day. I regret to say that there is no stop or pause on this bird.

If you are tempted to make a request, I would recommend sonnets. I think his temperament is just right for Petrarch. When he gets going, you'd think he really was in love. Or one of the nice little odes that Mr. Keats taught him. What a show he puts on for the sad parts, especially when he suspects that the poet is disappointed, as poor Johnny surely was. I got so tired of hearing about Fanny this and Fanny that.

—Say, just how old are you?

—That is not a proper question for *une femme de certain age*.

—Apologies. Does your bird have a name?

—We call him Amy. . . .

—Amy?

—After Amy Lowell, the American versifier and burlesque star.

—Good Christ! I had no idea she was a stripper!

—Anyhow, Amy-the-parrot could see right through Johnny's Shakespearian rhetoric to his testicular indignation, but, then, she is an animal. She gets that sort of thing. Yesterday she began crying while reciting Pope's "The Rape of the Lock." Now, that's a funny poem, I think, not a sad one, unless I'm missing something. I think the word "rape" threw her off. I suspect that the eighteenth century is completely lost on her. Parrots are strangers to irony.

—I like to cry till I laugh.

She gave me a "What does that mean?" look, an "out of left field" look. Then:

—How's the coffee?

—You know, I think it's perfectly balanced.

—Thank you, but you're wrong to say it's balanced. That would imply that there are conflicting elements within it. This particular brew is unconditioned (or "single-sourced," as your grocer might say, wrongly, but we do not expect our grocers to be metaphysicians). It is One. It has no qualities. In this coffee you taste only coffee's Suchness.

—Are you suggesting that this cup in my hands contains coffee's pure subjective infinity?

—That's right.

Believe it or not, this philosophical commentary on a cup of coffee was all very matter-of-fact for Felicité, like we were just talking about the appropriate blend of light and dark beans. But I was feeling playful, so I risked a riposte.

—To be honest, I think that your coffee is too complete. Coffee without conflict, unconditioned coffee, is dull. I prefer a synthetic resolution in my brew. Coffee with conditions is okay with me. That's why I put the hazelnut Coffee-mate in mine.

—Do you think I didn't notice? Do you always carry that awful stuff in your pocket?

—Yes, just in case. And a little Splenda. But I accept your criticism. It just shows why you are ethereal and otherworldly, and I am a mess. A wreck.

Felicité looked at me sadly and affectionately, much as she looked at Percy when he got into trouble. You'd think I really was a wreck. Then she looked at me some more.

—There's something odd about you, speaking of synthetic resolutions.

—What do you mean?

—I'm not sure how to put this, but has anyone ever suggested to you that you have a *cartoon* face? Do you remember Wimpy?

—Is that a joke?

—A joke? Cartoons *are* funny, so if there is a joke it is your own.

—My dear Queen, never mind that. Never mind cockatoos, long poems, the eighteenth century, coffee whether pure or synthetic, and, certainly, never mind my cartoon face. I have come to you for a reason. I have come to hear what you have to say about Percy. How *is* he? I have received questions about him. Some people want to know what he is exactly, and how you made him. Are there formulas? Could they make their own Percy at home? Or in college chemistry lab? Many of my readers are very technologically minded. They read novels as if they were reading *Popular Mechanics*, and I think that's a remarkable thing.

Others, the more naïve, perhaps, just want to know what happened to him. Has he adjusted to life back in bonny Islay? Did he find a girl? Settle down? Buy a home? Write a book? They don't like the ambiguity of his conclusion, and I can hardly blame them. How are they supposed to understand the stuff about being inside a snow globe? They feel as if they have been manipulated emotionally and then just allowed to fall to the floor, like poor Fanni. They feel that you have taken advantage of them. There's some resentment out there. In spite of everything, they came to care about Percy, to *love* him, in fact. I felt very much the same way.

—Oh, he's fine, the dear one. He's out on the front lawn now grazing among the spring flowers. He seems particularly fond of the crocus. He says that they are spicy.

—What? Percy? That doesn't sound like him at all! Grazing? He was becoming such a philosopher!

—Well, he *is* ruminating.

—This is terrible! None of my readers is going to like this if it's true! As I said, they really came to care about him, just as if he were a family member. He reminds some people of their own children. But now he's more like a distant uncle doing twenty to life out on the old chain gang.

—Which is why I've always said that readers are idiots. You are the one who has played them a dirty trick, I think. You've led them on and now you expect me to pick up the pieces for you. All I have to say is this: Percy is nothing special. He's just Percy, and he's *my* business.

—Come on! That's not fair! He was bright with intelligence and now you describe him as if he were a migrant doing lawn care . . . or a goat!

—When we returned from N—, I decided to give him a period of rest. He was getting into too much trouble, and many of his thoughts were . . . incorrect. You could see that yourself. All that malarkey about living with dogs! The weird orgy fantasies with teenaged girls and platinum-blond suburbanites and ex-cons! I mean, one can only hope he was making it up. And I sure didn't want him to come home all alienated and introspective and morbid like a ceramic Hamlet. I'd been through enough with him. He needed to have his faith in the simple things of the world restored. Yes, things like grass. Flowers. Dirt. He had become so *abstract*. I also felt he needed to have his trust in hierarchy and authority restored. As for your readers . . . do you actually have any? I mean, have you ever seen even one? Or is that just something you throw around to impress people?

—You know a Queen of Spells could just as easily be a Prince of Potions.

She gave me a terrible look.

—And a novelist can munch on grass!

—Touché! Actually, this is my first novel.

—*Is* it?

—I'm better known as a librettist.

—*Are* you?

—I met Philip Glass in 1970 on the steps outside Holly Solomon's gallery in SoHo. He was smoking a cigarette with David Bowie and a young Nicolas Africano. That was when I pitched my idea for an opera to him.

—Opera?

—That's what he said! You could see that the idea intrigued him. He asked what I had in mind. I said that the libretto I was working on was called "Autophagy: A Tragedy." Very stern, masculine, and Greekish. I said his austere music was perfect for it. Here was a story told at a cellular level. Cells break down their own components in response to nutrient deprivation and in order to keep the lights on *eat themselves*. I mean, if that isn't modern operatic material, I don't know what is. Think about the costumes! Naturally, as they eat, the cells become more and more *minimal*, just like his music. The whole thing, I said, was a metaphor for the slow self-consumption of Western culture. He really liked the idea, but he thought it should have three acts. But where do you go from there? I was stymied. I worked on it for months and then along came *Einstein on the Beach*, the sneaky bastard, and that stole my thunder. He got caught up in the hype, and now he might as well be composing radio jingles.

—Mm-hmmm. You know, I think *you* could use a period of rest.

—How's that?

—Never mind. Well, I don't have anything to say about your opera that it doesn't already say about itself, so, to return to Percy, if you're worried about him just look out the window. He's down there now cropping the lawn. This is Tuesday so he's probably doing some edging.

I did as she suggested, and there he was, like old Nebuchadnezzar, munching the growing green. The Queen had always seemed so nice. But this? I will admit, it made me anxious for my own safety.

—Well? Does he look like he's suffering?

—No, but he doesn't seem much like Percy either.

—Oh, Percy! I sometimes think you're as clueless as your stupid readers. What is a Percy, after all? A *character*? Frankly, for any human purpose, he lacks character. He, like you, is more on the order of a cartoon, or a puppet, or luggage.

—That's exactly what I came here to find out—what Percy *is*.

She sat back in her chair, put her fingers to her chin, as you see people do when they want to look like: "I'm thinking." And she really was thinking. She was wondering about the capacity of the vessel—me—before her. And who could blame her for that?

31.

"[Animals] do not just stand idly in front of sensuous things as if these possessed intrinsic being, but, despairing of their reality, and in complete certainty of their nothingness, they fall to without ceremony and eat them up."

—HEGEL

"And what are those little creatures grazing beside Percy?"

The Queen came to the window and looked down on the lawn.

"Oh, those are guinea pigs."

"Guinea pigs? They look like babies. Human babies."

"Yes. They do, don't they."

"So are these just more of your little creations?"

"No. They are Nature's creation."

"I'm sorry, but I'm a little confused. How can guinea pigs look like human babies on all fours?"

"It is interesting. As I understand it from newspaper articles I've read, guinea pigs were introduced into Scotland as pets in the late eighteenth century by Portuguese coffee merchants, with an eye toward product diversification, I suppose. In most places, they're just guinea pigs early and late, but here on Islay something happened. Some of the pets naturalized and spread rapidly. Then, especially in residential areas of the island, people began to notice little herds of what looked like infants calmly sitting together and munching on front lawns. Obviously, people were horrified at first and ran to pick the babies up and take them inside. But to their amazement, the little creatures scampered off into the forest."

I looked at her, my mouth open so wide that my perplexed

mind felt like it was dripping from my tongue. All I could manage to say was:

"This is impossible."

"No, this is Islay. We're isolated, just like the Galapagos. Things have an odd way of evolving here."

"My God!"

"Oh come! It's not unlike domesticated dogs, is it? You know how they can give those sad-eyed looks that appeal to something parental in us? Something that says to us, 'Give me food'? Give it another can of Chef Michael's Canine Cuisine Veal Marsala even if it is twenty pounds overweight and can barely waddle out to 'go potty.' The guinea pigs have just taken the next step. They're domesticated. These babies are actually a kind of emotional parasite. We offer them food and protection because it's impossible for us not to think that they really are babies. I'm quite serious. If you trap one—carefully!—it will sit in your lap and gurgle and coo. They parasitize our tender feelings and then get plenty to eat. People have offered bottles of formula to them, but they always throw them down and head for the cat kibble."

"How do you know they are even guinea pigs?"

"It's obvious, isn't it? Some kids trapped young pigs and put them in a cage. When they were about six months old, the children came out to feed them and there they were. Babies. Crying babies, too, because they expand at 'birth,' the moment when, like butterfly larvae, they metamorphose into baby form. They were jammed painfully against the cage's wire mesh and had to be cut out."

"Do they just continue to grow? Do they go to school? College?"

"Oh no. No, no. They have a very short lifespan. The metamorphosis is quite traumatic for the creatures. They live, usually, to be about two, two-and-a-half years old. Then, you know, they're rodents. They roll over, stick their legs in the air, and die."

"I'm feeling a little ill."

"Oh, you're just like the others around here. Some women, especially childless women, are never able to achieve emotional distance. Sure, you can say, 'They're only guinea pigs,' but they just don't understand. I understand the science of what has happened here, evolution, the logic of parasitism, genetic mutation and all that. But some folks just can't process it. The ocular evidence is just too strong."

"I can see why."

"The really tough times are when we experience population explosions and, inevitably, population busts. Like other rodents, they can outbreed their food sources. I suppose we could just start dumping bags of dog food out on lawns that they've chewed to the root, but that just increases the magnitude of the problem, doesn't it? Eventually, Islay would be coast-to-sorry-coast guinea-pig babies. And think of the consequences for the local ecosystem. It would be a puling desert. A baby monoculture. I don't even know that there would be room for us regular humans. So, we just have to let Nature take its course."

"I need to sit down."

"When these population crashes get really bad, some people can't even leave the house for fear of what they'll see. But even in times of stable growth there is always road kill. That's hard to take even for me."

"That image is not going to leave my brain for a very long time."

"I'm sorry, you sensitive thing you. Let me just conclude with two observations, one good, one very bad. First, no one has had to mow a lawn in years. Lawn-care people aren't happy about it, but homeowners sure are. Second, on the bad side (and I believe that this will shortly lead to legislation calling for the extermination of all guinea pigs on the island), there have been reported cases of infanticide in which the murdered child's body has been stripped and thrown out in an area with a large guinea pig population. Evil, but very difficult to detect without DNA lab work. You can imagine how the police feel when sifting through all the little corpses. And the labs hate doing autopsies on rodents. That's not what they signed on for."

"Please, stop."

"These murders, I believe, will spell the end of this little evolutionary experiment. I think they're doomed to be one of Nature's dead ends. Between the lawn-maintenance lobby and the concerns of law enforcement, you may be seeing the last of them now. So you might want to take a selfie with the creatures in the background. That will light up social media, won't it? Not to mention the bump in tourism that follows. I mean, people will want to see these things before they're all gone.

"But I do worry about Percy. I think he's become quite fond of them. I think he finds them comforting. I won't say I think he's right in this, but I think he feels that he has a lot in common with them. I know he'll be sad when they're gone."

Then the Queen looked at me and made a funny sort of face, and said, "Much sadder than I'll be when you're gone."

32.

"The medulla oblongata is a very serious and lovely object."

—FREUD

The medulla oblongata is a serious thing . . . if you've got one! When the Queen made that "funny sort of face," wrinkling her nose, there was a moment in which I wondered if she were taking mine. Staying awake, or just breathing, became a challenge. But I continued gamely.

"Do you know why the Portuguese coffee traders brought guinea pigs with them?"

"No, I don't."

"Did they carry them in their capacious Portuguese pockets, so popular in the day?"

"I don't know."

"Were the guinea pigs part of the trade? Or just companion pets during the long voyage?"

"Again, I don't know."

"Were they what you call a sales incentive? Buy this much coffee and get a free guinea pig?"

"That is not an unreasonable guess. Silly, but not unreasonable. But, once more and for the last time, I don't know."

"Or were they what are called 'loss leaders?'"

"*I don't know!!*"

"But *I'd* like to know."

"That, I'm afraid, cannot be in these circumstances."

"Have you ever thought about how many things are not known? I think that if someone made an honest, good-faith survey of the field of things known and unknown, the results would be distressing. I've come to believe that our proud knowledge accounts only for the smallest, most pathetic percentage of things that can be known. And if you throw in the things that are inaccessible to our proud perception, the percentage drops to the point where, statistically, you'd be tempted to say that we don't know anything at all."

"Please, stop."

"Here's what I'm saying. Let's take these trees here. We know, our knowledge boys and girls know, that something called sap flows up the outside, the so-called living perimeter, of a tree. If you've not seen it, I can tell you that it's right below the so-called bark. Up it flows and out through the leaves, where a fine mist of the stuff, or even heavy drops, then rain down like maple syrup on my car, ruining the paint job. Perhaps I notice that the drops form a non-pattern on the hood that I believe is called a 'random walk' in physics. Okay. My point is, why doesn't that readily accessible stuff, these things-of-the-world, rise to the level of knowledge?"

"Stop."

"Now, listen! The important point here is more than scientific. Who gets to say where the knowledge border is? Who gets to say that these things over here count as knowledge, but these other equally real things don't? Oh, those things over there, they say, are trivial. But I say nothing is trivial! The bag we call 'trivial' is stuffed with ninety-nine-point-nine-nine-nine-nine percent of knowable things. And I say that that just won't do."

"I'm warning you!"

"There is also the 'generality' question. Why is everyone so content with knowledge as a generality, a sort of schematic for negotiating the world? So what if it's practical, so what if the math works? I don't respect it. For example, we have the principle of photosynthesis, and we have drawings in high school textbooks with arrows showing the sun-soaked leaves converting the sun's rays into sugars, but what we should want to know is how this leaf, this leaf right here, steeps in warm light. I don't want a diagram. I want to know what it's like to be a leaf steeping in warm light and making sugar. There's something that it's like to be a leaf, agreed? I want to know what that is, what it's like. In essence, I want to *be* the leaf soaking right there, even if for just a moment. And then the same for every leaf on every tree everywhere. Now, *that* is what I call knowledge. Is that too much to ask? That's what we should want from knowledge, but that's not what we get. No, all we get is the executive summary."

"I was going to threaten to put you out with Percy if you didn't stop, but, actually, that's a good point and very well put. That 'executive summary' bit."

I "beamed," and once again language mocked itself painfully.

"And so, for the issue before us, it is shameful that we don't know why the Portuguese brought the guinea pigs to Islay. But that is such a gross oversight that it is tantamount to indifference. Supine galactic indifference. Was there no one at that time interested in a little research trip—paid for by his or her employer or written off as a business expense—to Lisbon for a look at the archival record? And there it would be in some ledger, the neat little columns, 'Import from the colonies: 271 guinea pigs'! And maybe there's a letter in which some guy in marketing takes credit for the idea: free guinea pigs will increase sales, especially among the poor, besotted folk of Scotland."

"Objection noted, but let me ask you in all candor, don't you think you need a little rest? I mean, my goodness, this can't go on, can it? You'll hurt yourself."

"A rest?"

"For your own good, sweetie. A period of rest."

"And that's just the beginning of it. Why don't we want to know if it was hard for the furry creatures to breathe in the capacious pockets of the Portuguese merchants? Why? I would not only like to know that, I would like to know what the oxygen, each molecule, was like in the guinea pig's blood. There's something that it's like to be a molecule of oxygen in a guinea pig's blood. Is that completely without interest for us? And everyone wants to know about the furry softness of the creature in the rough Portuguese hands. Did the tender softness of one of

God's creatures cause in the sailor a corresponding softening of heart? Did the sailor's tender feelings for the soft creature lead him away from his habit of molesting the lassies of Scotland? Who wouldn't want to know this?"

"Now I think you've gone dangerously far. What you say is something for God alone."

"Oh. I hadn't thought of that. So, it's up to God to sweat the small stuff? To know about the oxygen molecules and the long-ago molesting of lassies?"

"Exactly."

"Really, that is some comfort."

"I'm glad you think so."

"In that case, I would simply like to know if there are ever gaps in God's data stream. Does God nod?"

"As I said, this line of thought will get you into trouble on Islay. The Portuguese also brought the *auto da fé* with them, and as far as I know it's still a community resource in extreme cases. This has the feel of extremity."

"I'm sorry. Just let me say this, then: I love guinea pigs."

"That's nice."

"They're really cute."

"Yes, they are."

"And soft too."

I folded my hands in my lap, looked to the side, to the amber light of Scottish evening, each massless photon of it, flowing in the window. My lower lip trembled. There's something that it's like to have a lower lip tremble. I wiped at my eye, smearing the trees on the other side of the road. They fell all limp and blocked the little road down to the highway, as if they were only spaghetti trees.

Our kind Queen offered me a Kleenex from a family-sized carton printed in flowers of an indeterminate species done up in very pale pastel pinks and greens. I blew my nose and wiped my eyes, but it was too late for the trees and indeed for the road itself, which had gone all muddy, like a mountain road in a flood somewhere on a hill in Tennessee. The Kleenex carton smelled of cardboard. Cardboard is a paper product. As such, it was once a tree or even hundreds of trees. The trees need the sun and minerals and lots of water, which is abundant here for good or bad. The carton is the lumber company and its many employees and the many willing hands at the paper factory. Steam from the exhaust chimneys rises whitely against a stark blue sky. This all happens, as you well know, on Earth, third planet from the sun for the nonce.

The Queen of Spells reached a sober index finger toward me and touched my forehead.

33.

$$\text{The poetic ideal} = \sqrt[\frac{1}{0}]{\frac{FSM^{\frac{1}{0}}}{0}} = \text{God} \qquad \text{—SCHLEGEL}$$

When I woke up the next morning, I was stretched out on the Queen's front lawn. How did I get there? Had I humiliated myself (again!) by going one boilermaker over the line? (I should have known better than to drink the Queen's damned fairy bourbon.) But I didn't feel hungover, although I did have a funny taste in my mouth.

I got up and woozily walked toward the front door, composing embarrassed apologies as I walked, but the door was locked, and no one came when I knocked. I looked back across the lawn hoping to see Percy, but he wasn't there. (Probably off to winter pasturage.) And of course there was not a guinea pig or a baby-lookin' rodent in sight. What a crock that one was! And I'd believed it!

After trying every door and peering through every window, I decided that if I wanted some breakfast I was going to have to go somewhere else. I had a flight home that afternoon from little Benbecula Airport, but the Queen was supposed to transport me. Transport. That was the word she used. Did she mean that she would drive me in a car? I hadn't seen a car on her property. Did she mean some form of public transport? Did she assume I knew how or where to catch a bus? Or did she mean in some literal, black-magical way "transport"? I admit I started to panic, so I took a deep breath and walked down the steep drive toward the highway, maybe a quarter of a mile away.

When I got to the highway a vehicle was waiting. It looked like a horse-drawn coach without horses, but it didn't appear to have a motor of any kind either, or a driver. Must have been a Google prototype. There was something both old- and newfangled about it. I opened the door, and was just about to ask a passenger if this was a shuttle service to the airport when the damn thing took off and I was forced to leap inside or be stranded behind.

"This is more of the Queen's funny business," I said to myself.

There was only one other passenger, and he was sitting opposite me. He was dressed like an extra in a Charles Dickens Victorian costume drama, something BBC-y, comical and lugubrious. I could only see the top of his head because his face was buried in his hands. His long, thin, yet muscular fingers looked like roots digging into his skull. There was something monumental about him. It was like a companion sculpture to "The Thinker" called "The Sufferer," as if thinking wasn't suffering enough!

"Let him be," I thought. Just as I was thinking this, an image came to me. I remembered last night! With Félicité! I remembered that I had rudely fallen asleep. This was a lot worse than snoring during a college lecture. Everyone snored at those. But I had come a long way to sit at her feet . . . only to nod off! Had I missed something? Had she explained the mysteries of the cosmos and I had snored right through it? I groaned. How angry she must have been at my Gomer routine. Americans! No wonder I woke up on the lawn.

The man looked up when he heard me groan. I had never before seen a face so full of such concentrated pain. I could see that he was older, mid-forties, I'd say, but he was probably handsome when his face was not a gnarled sphincter of agony.

"Did you say something?" he asked. "Did I hear you groan? Are you, too, in pain?"

"I'm sorry to disturb you. I did groan. Please forgive me. It was a private thought. Don't be concerned."

At this the muscles in his face relaxed just a little.

"Ah, you, too, are one of the wounded," he said.

"That depends on whether or not I catch my flight."

"Flight?"

He asked as if I might be a migrating waterfowl. But then again, some folks did fly on the Isle of Islay.

"In an airplane," I assured him.

I think he suspected I was making fun of him, because the vortex of twisted muscles in the center of his face slid angrily to the side, a hideous thing to see.

"Sir, you mock me!"

"I don't mean to mock you. Why would I?"

"Because I deserve mockery. I wish you *would* mock me. The world should mock me. I am a fool."

This conversation was becoming as weird as the one I'd had with the Queen, but not so sleepy-making.

I said, "Do you mind my asking if you're okay? Is there any way I can help?"

"That is very kind of you. Perhaps you can."

Then he looked at me intently, as if for the first time. The twisted muscles that had moved to the side of his face relaxed back to the center, like pudding flowing.

He said, "That is a very odd sort of face you have."

He should talk!

"I beg your pardon?"

"It makes me feel like laughing. Do you know the cartoon Winky the Wanker?"

I scowled.

"No, I don't. And I don't think I'd like to know."

"No offense, sir. It's just a cartoon popular in our pubs. The lads like it for a larf. I'm sorry. Now I've hurt your feelings. Forget I said anything. Because I need you, friend. I must ask you to listen to what I've done. We have a long journey before us. Perhaps if I could talk about what is tormenting me, I'd be in less pain. Is there a chance you could verify that the things I've experienced are things that other humans experience? I feel so alone with my flaws and sins. Perhaps you could even tell me if I've done wrong? What is my crime? What my punishment?"

"Another moron," I thought, wondering if his private hell was like everybody else's. I could tell him the answer to that now. There is no private hell. Just hell. Just this prison. But I tried to be tactful.

"I'm no therapist, but I'd be willing to listen."

I was stuck in this cab alone with a madman. What was I supposed to say? Maybe I could mug him for authentic human details that I could use in my novel.

"Oh, thank you. Thank you."

"One thing before you begin: There aren't any guinea pigs in your story, are there? Stories with guinea pigs put me to sleep."

34.

"The will acts in proportion to its fancied power, to its superiority over immediate obstacles. The being baulked of this throws the mind off its balance, or puts it into what is called a passion; and as nothing but an act of voluntary power still seems necessary to get rid of every impediment, we indulge our violence more and more, and heighten our impatience by degrees into a sort of frenzy."

—HAZLITT

I felt a little guilty taking his thanks because, you know me, I had every intention of stealing his story if it was good, assuming that he didn't ruin it by telling me too much.

He began circumspectly.

"Do you know about computers?"

I thought he was kidding.

"I mean those computers that are called *personal*?"

"Yes, I know about them."

"Here in Islay, not only men but also women are allowed to own and use them."

"That is the same for us in the United States."

"Really? Even there, in that enlightened place?" He seemed both surprised and intimidated by the idea. "But there are so many women there."

"Roughly fifty-fifty, I'd guess."

He seemed to do some quick calculations, peering into some

appalling potentiality, his hands once again on his head, pulling at his hair this time. "How awful!" he concluded.

I had to laugh just a little, which didn't help his mood.

"Here in Islay the personal computer, especially its use by women, is new. I wish to God that it had never come to pass, but our legislature in a moment of mistaken liberality forgot what has made our island great. But I admit that I am conservative by nature. Even in my youth I objected when women were allowed to go about without gunny bags over their heads. Frankly, even though I was only ten at the time, I argued that men and women should both have to wear the bags. I went so far as to parade around town wearing one myself, just to make the point. Of course, I was laughed at, but we have seen what we have seen, haven't we?"

Whatever that meant.

"At first when we brought the computers into our homes we put them, as is our custom with other things dangerous to women and children—car keys, guns, newspapers—in locked rooms. Unfortunately, you could see the soft glow of the computers through outside windows. The women were mesmerized by it. Both women and children began to gather outside, looking longingly at the penumbra. You'd have thought it was a shrine for the virgin and miracles were expected." He looked down angrily. "That's when I put the 'Women are requested not to linger in this area' sign up, for which I suffered the most unfair abuse."

He looked into some very dark and very personal inner space lit only by the luminous eyes of demons.

I said, "Don't take this wrong, because I understand where you're coming from, but have you never heard of equal rights?"

He looked at me, mouth wide, a look of confusion and something like despair in his eyes.

"That's all right," I consoled, "I never thought much of them—the equal rights—myself."

Finally, he gathered himself.

"Sir, I have never beaten a woman!"

"That's helpful to know."

His liquid emotions were more somber now, you know, introspective stuff, like he was running over the events of his life just to be sure about his claim regarding beating women.

"I've never beaten one, although they readily provide just cause for beatings. As for the computers, I should have known that we couldn't keep them out of their hands forever."

"But," I objected, "some of your most powerful people are women. I have a particular friend here, Felicité, Queen of Spells, and she is truly a force to be reckoned with."

"You know the Queen of Spells?"

"Yes, I do."

He looked lost in an infinite confusion and said, "That is another matter entirely, I assure you."

Then he began to tell his story. I'll spare you the lengthy version of his particular moral destruction, the slow dissolve of his life. It was the usual story of the May/December marriage, technically updated. Once women were granted access to personal computers, his young wife, some twenty years his junior, did what was inevitable. She began posting thrilling photographs of herself on various websites. Repairmen were attracted to the sites. His young wife finally ran off with the "odd-job fella," as she called him.

Oh, you should've heard him go on about it all. It was ridiculous. You'd think it was something out of the ordinary, and maybe in backward Islay it was. Still, I thought, his story really did offer a promising subject for a novel, done in the right way. It immediately started shaping itself in my mind: set in rural Illinois. A young wife brings the handyman home for the husband's pizza, and together the three of them embark on an exciting and profitable amateur porn site. She floats a stock option in the second year, and a majority of the shares are purchased by Russian venture capitalists. Romanian mafia and Shabab terrorists begin hanging out in the TV room, looking out for their investments. Things get dicey when the husband fails to maintain an erection and is threatened by a Somali extremist with a scimitar, the scimitar being, of course, the reason for his flaccid member.

Promising, but back to present things.

Strangely, my companion's missing wife wasn't at all the reason for his present condition. In the last few weeks they'd negotiated—via Skype—a compromise. She could watch "Ooooh!" and other cute kitten sites, and he would no longer threaten to have her stoned by his family. In fact, she'd already apologized for her behavior and was at that very moment traveling home to be with him once again.

"Well, if that's the case, what in the world are you doing here? Why aren't you home waiting for her? Making a quiet little dinner. Chilling a pleasant little bottle of Galway blush."

Once again he resorted to the head-in-the-hands routine, the fingers digging down into his skull like fusiform tubers.

"There is no home," he confessed. "I burned it to the ground."

35.

"My hopped up husband drops his home disputes,
and hits the streets to cruise for prostitutes,
free-lancing out along the razor's edge.
This screwball might kill his wife, then take the pledge."

—ROBERT LOWELL,
"TO SPEAK OF WOE THAT IS IN MARRIAGE"

"What? You burned your own house down? I don't know who has been counseling you on this point, but that is *not* the way to a woman's heart."

That seemed like sound advice to me, but he looked ready to burst out either angrily or in tears or in angry tears.

He settled for saying, "It was beyond my control."

"If you could restrain yourself from beating women, why couldn't you restrain yourself from committing arson on your own home? Belongings too? I suppose the computer went up."

"Yes, the computer's destruction is the only part I don't entirely regret. But I was not thinking of it at all when I poured on the accelerant and lit the match."

Looking out the window of our strange conveyance, I saw a sign indicating that the airport was only a few kilometers away.

"Well, I suppose there was a reason whether good or bad, but I'm afraid I won't have time to hear it. I'll be getting off at the airport. Then Glasgow and the sweet United States."

"Ah! The United States! Surely women never do these filthy things there."

"Never."

"How good! But still, you must listen!"

What I hadn't anticipated was my companion throwing himself to his knees before me, clasping his hands, and looking up imploringly.

"What I've told you is just prologue. I need to tell the whole story, but if you won't listen I'm afraid I'll never have the courage to start again!"

"Get on with it then, man!"

I guess I was a little petulant. I hadn't eaten breakfast or had my morning coffee. I was perhaps a little hypoglycemic. I saw that my clothes were torn and grass-stained. Looking at my dim reflection in the window, I saw that clumps of straw were sticking out of my hair. I couldn't go to the airport like this! And what about my luggage? I felt for my wallet. Thank God it was there or I think I'd have torn the coach door from its hinges and leaped out, screaming, onto the highway.

"Come on, man!" I yelled, "I don't have all day!"

Pity I didn't have a scimitar.

"Okay, okay! Let's see. As you suggested, when my wife told me that she would return and was even eager to see me, I was very happy. Our separation had been the single greatest crisis of my life. After a lifetime of disappointments, to fail now, in this humiliating way, was more than I could bear. I was so calm, so determined, so patient, so stoic, and, in spite of it all, quietly confident that I could get her back. My friends and colleagues were amazed at how focused I was. And don't think my wife wasn't impressed. She was. Once, after one of our last Skype negotiations, she looked deeply into her computer monitor and said, 'You have changed. You really have changed.'"

I don't know what gave her that impression!

"So I did in fact begin to prepare a celebratory meal for us. It was short notice, and I felt a little hurried, but I thought I could throw something nice together if I didn't get too complicated. I knew I had a bag of mushrooms harvested from a nearby forest, chicken, cream, pasta, and a bottle of the local rosé. I could do it.

"So I went quickly to the kitchen and looked for the mushrooms. Unfortunately, they'd been in the cooler a little longer than I remembered. They were all a suspect shade of black and a very inky fluid filled the bottom of the bag. I opened the pouch and smelled. Off, definitely off, but not completely rotten.

"So, okay, they'd be fine in a sauce. That's what sauces are for. But when I reached for the butter there was only a note from my neighbor acknowledging that he'd borrowed the butter—two weeks before! All right, I'd cook the mushrooms in oil. I then reached for the little pitcher of cream. Empty. I had put the cream back in the icebox empty. I remember my wife's complaints about my habit of putting empty containers back into the icebox so that reaching for anything was like playing a very low-stakes version of Russian roulette. 'So,' I thought, 'maybe I can substitute yoghurt.' It was fat-free, and flavored with vanilla, but better than nothing. Tragically, except for some drooly whey at the bottom, the yoghurt too was empty. No wonder she got so angry. 'Well,' I thought, 'I'll just use this powdered buttermilk. Maybe that will work.'

"By this time, my frustration and irritation were starting to build. So, I thought that a small glass of the wine was in order. Sit down, have a drink, then return to dinner preparation. But that was not to be. I went to pull the cork, and it slipped out with a sickening squishy plop.

"Well, now I was upset. In the course of the next half-hour, I drank the bottle of bad rosé. Then I drank a quart of beer that I had stoppered the week before. When I finished, I of course was not seeing much of anything correctly. The living room was fuzzy. But like a little window of clarity cut into the center of the fuzz I could see in perfect detail my wife's lovely face sinking in disappointment, looking at this meal, looking at her drunk husband, wondering if coming home had really been such a good idea.

"But I hadn't given up. Properly herbed, the meal could still be a winner. 'Tarragon,' I thought. 'Tarragon will pull this all together.' I went to the sliding herb drawer and pulled. The drawer moved out by one-eighth of an inch and stopped. Something, a bottle of turmeric, had fallen sideways and was blocking it. Worse, it seemed to be well back where not even the blade of a knife could reach it.

"Furious, I pulled again. Then harder. *Harder yet!* It was at that point that a fuse in my head went off, and my mind with it. I put my foot against the counter and threw the full force of my body into it. The herb drawer and a side of the cabinet frame exploded outward. Tins of mustard, dill seed, curry, oregano went crashing in every direction. I looked at my hand. It still held the drawer knob.

"'So,' I said to myself, 'you've broken the drawer. Well, if you've broken one drawer, you might as well break them all!' Believe it or not, in that moment that felt like a sunny idea. So I did. I destroyed every drawer, destroyed every cabinet and countertop. I pushed the fridge over and even used a chunk of maple butcher block to devastate the sink and its plumbing. The kitchen started to fill with water."

"I know exactly how you felt."

"It gets a little crazy now. I thought, 'You can't have her find this mess. She'll turn tail and go back to her handyman.'"

"So you burned the whole house down."

"I did."

"That *was* a triumph."

"I won't lie to you, it felt really good."

"But then . . . "

"Right. But then, standing on the front lawn, looking at the flames shooting up through the roof, sirens nearing, I realized what I'd done. And I realized that I couldn't be there when she arrived. I just couldn't. I couldn't face it."

"So you ran away and here, by God, you are."

"Yes."

"And that was all yesterday evening?"

"I'm afraid so."

"Nice job!"

A little low moaning.

"I don't know if it has occurred to you, but when your wife comes back and finds the house burned to the ground, fire trucks milling around, a crowd of strangers laughing and drinking beer, and, the worst, no you . . . she's going to think it's all a message to her. Passive aggression on steroids. She's going to think you did it on purpose."

The idea stunned him.

"But it was . . . How could . . . Oh my God, what have I done?"

"Well, this is where I get off. Nice to meet you. Hope things work out for you and your wife."

36.

"Ohimé!"

—ORPHEUS, IN MONTEVERDI'S *ORFEO*

Once in the terminal, I went to a restroom before going to the counter. I brushed my clothes, washed my face and hands, and dampened my hair to get a comb through it. Even so, the mirror was unkind. I thought I looked like a woodsy mammal that had caught fire and then been stomped out. But that was going to have to do.

I went up to the counter of the regional airline and presented a credit card. The young woman behind the counter was smiling and professional. She was even professional about the way I smelled, bless her. But then, peering into the monitor, she frowned and said, "You are in our system, but the flight you were to take was ten days ago."

"Ten days ago?!"

"Yes." She laughed. "You missed your flight."

I freaked. I had important responsibilities back home. Jake, the Marquis of N—'s grandson, was on the road with that scapegrace Rory. In ten days Rory could have bollixed the trip in any number of regrettable ways. I had to be there. The Marquis would surely hold me responsible.

"Well, you still have a credit with us and we can book you from Glasgow back to the U.S. There will be a change fee of one hundred dollars, but your credit card is in good order. Shall I put the fee there?"

"Yes, please, but hurry!"

She became just a little terse. "How fast I go has no bearing on when your plane leaves. Your plane leaves when your plane leaves whether I hurry or not, and that's not for several more hours."

"I'm sorry," I said, "I'm just upset." I felt a little like taking the bus, or whatever that thing was, back to the Queen's and curling up on the lawn. Perhaps that was the life for me.

She started looking at me with suspicion. Here I was ten days late for a flight, I had no luggage, and no idea what day it was, my clothes were dirty and torn and tiny pieces of leaf were still stuck in my hair, and now I was behaving suspiciously.

She handed me a ticket and said, "Have a nice flight," but before I could turn around I felt a tap on my shoulder. A man in a dark suit stood there with two armed security men behind him.

"Sir? Come this way with us, please."

How easy it is to become a "person of interest" these days. But then I'd always wanted to be interesting.

37.

"Only the artist is capable of redeeming society...but that order is so wrong that the very effort of the artist recoils upon itself and destroys him."

—MORSE PECKHAM

By the time I got back to the Midwest, Jake and Rory were in the lake country of northern Minnesota. I had never intended that they go so far north. On old bicycles no less. I have no idea what happened to the horses I gave them. I guess the willing suspension of disbelief was willingly suspended on the road somewhere between N— and Madison. Maybe I'd been gone so long they just forgot the horses. They woke up one day and, in that demoralizing derangement we call morning, got on bikes instead of trusty steeds and never noticed afterward. That disappoints me just a little. I thought they were better than that.

And of course the plot that I had so carefully crafted was impossible now. Those wonderful narrative devices Rory had brought along? Well, you can forget them. They lost their fragment of the map. The letter had fallen into a puddle during a rainstorm, the lottery ticket with it. Even the gun was gone. They sold it, under duress, to a gang of dogs not far north of N—. The dogs claimed they needed it to get even with a "certain Alpha." Worse yet, our boys had to accept dog money for it, delivered in an enormous bale, like something to feed cattle with in the winter.

Jake said, "Maybe we should have hung on to the gun until they showed us real money."

Rory said, "Doesn't matter. Those bullets I gave them are not investment grade. They are junk-bond bullets. Just pray we're not around when the dogs find out."

Jake shrugged. What did he know about junk bonds?

Rory cursed, threw the bale of dog dollars into the campfire, and went to Jake's tent. He was done explaining things to Jake for that day.

The bale just smoldered.

Completely lacking in guidance, they kept pedaling north looking for a job, whatever that could mean by this point. Let's face it, all that was left to them was entropy; they'd spent energy, lots, and done a job of work, but with horrible inefficiency, and now all that remained was a kind of pollution, the smoggy miasma that followed their many failures.

But now that, at last, we can rejoin our friends, I have to say that they are in a wondrous place in spite of it all.

Just look!

38.

"Fuck me, I'm falling apart."

—SUFJAN STEVENS

Jake and Rory were walking their bicycles, still heading north. They were sad, I suppose, but it was not an unpleasant sadness. I think they'd grown used to the daily routines of their trek, even the suffering. There was something both simplifying and satisfying about it all. The trip had become a kind of pilgrimage, even if it was a pilgrimage without a destination or even a purpose. They had long ago forgotten about the job search.

But, ah!, Minnesota! The road moved between high peaks, stark and treeless, carved by gale force winds. Peat bogs in deep tarns marked the upland fallows. Streams moseyed across rumpled moraines. Ice Age fish endured at the bottom of the cold lakes. Footpaths followed the ancient Roman trade and military routes. They walked along narrow lanes, and close by thickly lichened walls tufted with wallflowers and encrusted by hedges. All was black and sullen, and yet alive with an inaudible motion, as if the scene were one living thing, a spirit.

From a rocky crest they looked northeast into a valley where a vast reservoir shimmered. The rocky path was treacherous and slick from centuries of human travel, the steep sloping ground was soaked from last night's rain, but at last they arrived at a lake (Lake Mandubracius, in case you know it) where a stand of ancient oaks and enormous boulders (they kept the state from floating away) created a sort of living space, a theater, a place for human gestures.

There before them was an artist, a painter, with his easel, looking out toward the copse and, spreading to the horizon, the lake. He had his back to them and was concentrating on his work. A hat of fine woven fibers, linen and hemp, bobbed as he looked from trees to lake and back to his canvas. Jake and Rory approached him with deep respect, just as they had done so many times before, in so many places, all of which must here remain blank pages. Finally, they were standing right behind him, quietly, shy about disturbing him, knowing how important his work was to the maintenance of Things.

But you know Rory by now. The parakeet in him could stand the silence only so long.

"Hi, there," he said, too loudly and too close.

The artist was startled and turned quickly.

"Oh, you scared me," he said, laughing.

"Sorry!" said Rory.

Like a child who is disappointed that a toad sits still and so pokes it with a stick, he wasn't sorry at all.

"Really," Jake said, "we are sorry. We don't want to disturb you."

"That's all right. I'm just sitting here in friendly strife with Nature. But I understand. A painter makes everything just a little uncomfortable."

"What do you mean?"

"I mean that artists make a scene like this, which only wants to be what it is, feel very self-conscious. The trees have the look of trees that know they're being looked at, and that's a problem for an artist. Surely you can see that the lake and the trees, the birds, even rocks and dirt are agitated. They'd like to run away and hide. Through the artist, Nature becomes bashful, as if discovered naked as Diana. The artist, for this affront, must try to move Nature's embarrassment to the other side, to dignity and nobility, before the dogs are sicced on him. In the end Nature thanks the artist because, after the indignity of being looked at, it understands for the first time that it is beautiful." He smiled a self-effacing smile. "Or that's what I think."

Rory was jumping up and down.

"Sir, I think we have a live one here."

Dubious, Jake asked, "May we look at your painting?"

"Certainly. Of course it's not done in its detail, but I have already seized what I set out to seize. I have wrested it from Nature. I don't yet know how the scene, especially the liquid lake, feels about it. At present, I believe it is encouraged, hopeful that it can at last become the lake that it is."

Our boys came closer as the artist scooted his little folding seat to the side. If, at that moment, you had looked from behind the painting at their faces, you would have seen them squint in incomprehension. Rory's face stayed like that, but Jake's face seemed to open in surprise, alarm, you might even say horror.

Rory, as usual, was the first to speak. "Your painting doesn't look much like what you're looking at, does it? You must be one of those modern painters."

The artist laughed. "No, no. It is just so."

They were quiet for a minute before Jake, looking stricken, asked, "Who is that woman?"

Rory looked again at the painting. "What woman?"

Speaking to Jake, the artist asked, "Do you mean who is my model?"

"Whatever you call her. How did she get here?"

"She's just a local girl."

Rory was now bouncing around from point to point, seeking an angle that would allow him to see what they were seeing.

"She is not a local girl." Jake froze, afraid to say what was so obvious to him, afraid that he would reveal himself as mad. "Rory, can't you see? That is Fanni. Sir, that is my ex-wife."

Now Rory was in a frenzy. Looking up, practically between the artist's legs, he said, "Now I see her, or something. Very like an ex-wife."

Jake didn't even have the self-control to tell Rory to shut up, so I'll have to do that for him.

"Oh, for God's sake, Rory, please shut up!"

"I assure you," said the artist, "she's just a country girl. A plump midwestern thing."

"That's impossible. That woman grew up in a condo in Aurora where drug dealers and pedophiles marched through her living room daily. There's nothing wholesome about her. She is damage itself."

The artist studied his own painting, just to reassure himself.

"I'm sorry, but unless you want me to say that my life has been one long hallucination, I can't agree with you. Besides, at this point she's just a cartoon. I haven't given her features, not even a nose. There's nothing to make you think she's anybody, let alone your ex-wife."

Jake turned to face the artist. It looked like he was going to knock his finely braided hat off. Bloody his nose. Challenge him to a duel. Who knows what? He was falling apart.

The artist was a little unnerved. "Look," he said, "would you like to meet her?"

39.

"When a man seeks his love, he'll take even a monster by the hand."

—GOETHE, *FAUST*

Then out from behind one of the monumental boulders came a young woman. She emerged as if she had been waiting just off-stage, in the curtains, for her cue. She was a plain woman, a little heavy-set, with a length of brown hair falling loosely around a pleasantly plump peasant's face made attractive by two deep dimples at the corners of her mouth. She also had lively, inquisitive, and playful eyes. She wore a loose pale-blue dress, belted at the waist, with buttons down the front.

She said to the artist, "Do you need me?"

It was as if she were at his beck and call, as if she had nothing better to do than loiter behind that boulder until called to the dull duties of a model.

Then she said, "Oh, I didn't know you had guests."

"'Zanne, these are travelers."

Her name was Suzanne, but her friends, and the artist was a friend, a real caregiver, called her "'Zanne."

"Welcome, then." She smiled beautifully!

Rory bounced up as if he were a Mouseketeer.

"Pleased to meet you. I'm Rory."

Jake was more reserved. I'm afraid he said nothing but only studied her. She felt his examination, and her face reddened and fell just a little.

Rory tried to help.

"Master Jake, your manners! I'm so sorry, miss, but he's been under a lot of stress. He is Jake, grandson to the Marquis of N—."

She said, "A mark key?"

Jake said, "Don't listen to him. I am nothing. Until just now, perhaps."

"What's that?" Rory exclaimed.

Jake looked to the artist and stated—it was almost a challenge—"This is not the woman in your painting. Thank God."

The artist was dumbstruck. When he began to explain, Jake cut him short.

"I don't want to hear your explanation. I am not stupid. I have been naïve, but I am not stupid. But I may be dangerously angry. First, you show me a painting with my ex-wife in it, a gratuitous insult to my still-raw feelings. Then, expecting to see Fanni come out from behind this boulder, I see this lovely girl . . . with whom I am quickly falling in love, even as I speak."

"No, my young friend, none of this is true. I think you may be in need of a period of rest," replied the artist, his face both wary and worried.

"He certainly is!" cried Rory.

40.

"If we are able to penetrate the exterior of things, we would see that the true stuff of life and existence is the horrible."

—SCHELLING

Before 'Zanne begins her story, I need to tell you something about the way that she told it. When she first emerged and joined the illuminated circle of our little group, she seemed all innocence. She was chastely dressed in a long cotton dress, with modest buttons in the front, and a spotless apron, a real working apron, as if we had interrupted her while she kneaded dough or milked a cow. I think you might want to call her a maiden. She was like a girl who had come forth in all simplicity, blameless and pure, from a sentimental engraving of the sort that decorated the modest homes of the candid German bourgeoisie in the nineteenth century. In that engraving, a girl crosses a stream flowing over pebbles, the mighty Black Forest behind, its darkness restrained by her chastity. A dog, a Saint Bernard, perhaps, stands faithfully by her side, his paws in the little creek. She glances back gracefully, as if the artist had caught her in the middle of a dance step. A faint, pure smile is on her lips, and she holds the hand of her baby brother, who staggers at her side barefoot on the slippery polished stones, but utterly trusting in his dear sister's care. She is impeccable, without sin.

This is how Jake first saw her, and once he'd seen her in this way nothing would ever persuade him to see her otherwise.

Of course, there is a problem with that sort of vision, however heartfelt it might be. Frankly, and I can give her full credit for frankness, she was no sentimentalist, and there was nothing about the way she told her story that should have encouraged Jake's way of seeing her. Unfortunately, this complexity of character was lost on Jake, but I heard it and noted it well.

I know that it must seem as if my characters live not in the world but midway in some interior distance, suspended between a mute God and the babble of the world. In short, my characters are curiously lacking in character. They are self-negating. This may sound abstruse, but I like the lack of clarity in this bracketed space between the ineffable and the incorrigible. It suits me.

But I recognize that not everyone feels this way. That oddball anachronism that we call the "Reading Public" would prefer that the bracket, where the Work says its piece, be in among the particulars of a *familiar* world. In other words, their little world. It should remind them of *family*, of *real places*, of, God forgive them, *real people*. I can hear them now, those weary voices who would simply like to say that the author ought to try to help out now and then. A time and a place, they say. Give us that. For instance, they suggest, Delhi, in 1943, the dying days of the British Raj. The viceroy's insomnia. The confusion and suffering among the sepoys of the Pankot rifles. The rich sentimentality for the old days when the colonialists were mother and father to a world of dark children.

Then, completely out of bounds, the Reading Public shouts, "Or at least can we have some trees?"*

I'm sorry, but much as I would like to oblige, to cooperate, to satisfy and comfort, I don't know anything about colonial India. In all honesty, I can't even say I know much about trees except to say that they seem to be all over the place. But the Reading Public should admit that I have committed myself to a few things. Minnesota, for example. That's a place. It's even a state. Also, a lake with a name: Lake Mandubracius (ridiculous, I admit, but I'm new to this). And there are boulders (about which I've already said too much). So, since it makes you happy, I will say something more about the trees. Writers often do. Only painters seem to enjoy them more, use them, profit from them in all sorts of ways. Musicians I think couldn't care less about trees. In fact, I suspect that most musicians are afraid of trees. Something about them. If only all of my readers were musicians, I'd be free of this obsession of the Reading Public!

I hope now that we can return to the wide-open spaces of the American interior, and I promise you solemnly, there will be trees, lots of trees.

---

* If you're wondering how I know what the Reading Public thinks: I have my literary agent to thank for that. She insisted that I "crowdsource" my creation before sending it to an editor. She explained that "if you test your book online, you can really tailor it to what people want to read." I couldn't argue with that.

41.

(IN WHICH READERS GET THE TREES THEY DESERVE)

"Science slanders matter."

—SCHELLING

—after Cormac McCarthy

From their camp at the crest of La Cordillera de los Arboles, they looked south toward Mexico, the vast Sonora, which was unbroken except for the dwarfish mesquite and chaparral that give the desert floor a fuzzy appearance, a world without qualities. About two miles out, a pickup truck sped west, like something in torment, a long spiral of dust growing broad and indefinite, a trailing thought too grim to finish.

Mexico was a past that had lost all promise, not least because the pickup was carrying four drug-gang foot soldiers with AKs and a grenade launcher that they were always eager to use, and, worse yet, they were trailing Jake and his little party. For the moment, thank God, they were off the track.

To the north, La Cordillera de los Arboles swooshed elegantly to the left, an enormous, rhythmic, comma-shaped line of pin oak and dry-green loblolly pine. They could just see where the comma's trail ended, a swale softly settling to a hard-green river bottom of bald cypress, soaking in a patch of wetland fed by a shallow river running over brightly-polished stones. They would need to get to the sanctuary of the cypress grove by the early afternoon if they wanted to avoid the *drogistas* and the worst of the heat. Once they got to the trees and the wetland, Rory could make a moss poultice for the nasty gash in Jake's shoulder, which was still oozing beneath the bandanna the girl had wrapped around it.

The girl was another kind of problem. She would slow them, but it couldn't be helped. After all, it was she they'd come for. Their boss had given them each a ten-dollar gold piece and nailed two more to a post, promising the money to them if they brought her home. He was called the Artist because of his imaginative knife-based talent for conflict resolution. What made this task difficult was that the girl loved those gangsters and their drugs, and she was none too happy about leaving them, especially since it meant returning to the Artist and his knife tricks. When she imagined him, he was pushing back his hat of fine-woven fibers, a black patch over his right eye, balancing a V-42 stiletto point on his index finger until a little drop of incarnadine blood puddled beneath it. The Mexicans were nurturers in comparison to the Artist.

As Jake saw it, if the horses held up, they'd make it to the trees. They could get water, then, in one of the clear ponds, full of darters and snails, up close to the river. The horses could eat the river grasses, and there'd be plenty of silver or rosy-eyed perch for dinner.

So, tired but dogged, they saddled the horses and cut the girl loose from her stake. She rubbed at the raw welts on her wrist but climbed quickly onto her horse without complaint. She was in withdrawal from one or more opioids, and so was starting to think that the best thing for her was to arrive some-where, anywhere. She was a hard girl after the long months in the criminal camp on the desert floor, and she'd seen her share of addicts piled on the ground, their bones clattering like castanets. She was a girl who paid attention and learned, Jake gave her that, but he also knew he'd have to treat her without pity. Pity was something he didn't have time for. So what if she had some bloody welts from the leather cords. Let her keep still, then.

They kept to the deer and boar path through the pines. It smelled wonderful, like rarest oxygen and dirt, dry and purged of every impurity. It was just simply World and it was so pleasant that it was distracting from their perilous task. At one point even Rory looked over at Jake and, well, he didn't smile, but he seemed to think about smiling, which was a lot for a man whose face looked more like a carved mask of some island god, the slits of his eyes hard against the sunset.

The grove of ancient cypress that awaited them was thriving side-by-side with the dwarf palmetto and a fairy world of dreamlike Spanish moss. The bark of the cypress is red-brown with shallow vertical fissures. Unlike most other species in the family *cupressaceae*, it is deciduous, hence the name "bald." The "knees" they send up above the water line add to their elderly charm. But for Rory and Jake, it was just shelter, a place to hide before the long, open, and dangerous ride toward the Palo Duro and then the little tobacco shop in Amarillo, where the Artist waited, whittling and whistling "Danny Boy."

The cypress swamps are home to marsh wren, bittern, and red crossbill, and, high in the trees themselves, barred owl and pileated woodpecker. Also, the ruddy ghost rail, a bird of legend. I linger on this point in order to determine more exactly the real character of trees and the nature of the comfort and aid they offer birds as well as, on that one day, our friends.

Looking up, Jake could see not only the birds but also small gray squirrels (upon which the cypress depends to spread its seeds). Both birds and squirrels were in numerous small wooden boxes obviously derivative of the boxed assemblages of found objects created by the American surrealist Joseph Cornell. The boxes were firmly and safely wedged into the "crotches" of the tree limbs. Jake couldn't help but marvel at them, never mind that his situation was so dire that he might not live to see the end of the day. Moreover, the full aesthetic impact of the boxes was lost on Jake, a man for whom everything was already surreal. It was the real that shocked him. And I think it was the real that he marveled at in those boxes full of bottle caps, a yellowed ping-pong ball, a lexicon for upholstery buttons printed on torn newsprint, things that jays might have brought and stored if Mr. Cornell hadn't taken care of it first. Come to think of it, the jays might have resented the intrusion into their job description. It is, after all, their job to steal buttons and such and hide them in little cubbyholes in trees. That is well established in both high school textbooks and peasant lore.

One of the little boxes was low enough that Jake could reach in and pull out the contents. He froze in horror. In his hand he held a bullet from a Sharps rifle Model 1851. That was the one with the knife-edge breechblock and self-cocking device for the box-lock. It was also the prized possession of one Alvaro "Chingé" Alvarez, he who the Chispés cartel depended on when death at a distance was called for. Model 1851 or no, Chingé never missed, and he was notorious for leaving one of his bullets, unmistakable, as an invitation to a death that was foretold and not far off. Jake did a quick pan of the surrounding hills. He palmed the spent cartridge when Rory came over to see what he'd found, although the stoic Rory would not have deigned to show alarm had he seen the shell.

For a moment, Jake thought that maybe they should spend the night there, but, on the other hand, whether they stayed or went, Jake feared that it was all one to Chingé. Wherever they went, he was already waiting.

For their part, the squirrels were no happier than the jays about Jake's meddling with their boxes. He had pulled a miscellany of seeds and nuts out with the bullet. The squirrels eat the many small green cones the bald cypress produces, and drop many of the scales with undamaged seeds to the ground. Germination is *epigeal*. Once on the ground, the seed takes its place with years of dry, frondlike leaves shed each winter by the deciduous cypress. This provides an ideal environment for germination.

While few people would think to do so, if one looks just beneath this cypress debris (easily swept aside), they will find a vast network of drips of liquid color, mostly alkyd enamels, spreading to the forest boundary in a sort of natural "all-over" style strikingly reminiscent of Jackson Pollock's No. Five, 1948, with its black base rising through brown and yellow to a white surface. A flute motif is provided by tubular, elongated, and thread-like filaments called hyphae of the *basidiomycete* fungi. (Of course, the filaments are a recent innovation by Nature, not by Mr. Pollock, and are part of a product line dating back to the Mesozoic, although those beneath Jake's boots were probably fungal apps released and then abandoned by Natquest.com in the late '90s—a very early example of digital pollution.)

Just beneath the colorful abstract expressionist surface—a very thin and sere layer of liquid colors—is the forest's mechanics, its ductwork, which provides for heating, ventilation, and cooling of the forest floor, and in a manner that both the business community and local environmentalists agree is sustainable. In places where forests have been cleared away, archaeologists have been able to dig carefully through the "Pollock" superstratum and expose Nature at her most ingenious. The forest itself may cause a warm feeling of distant admiration in a viewer, but to look upon what makes the forest work, a phenolic system of flexible fabric ducting (also known as "air socks"), is to see something truly rare. It is no wonder that Nature is so often called a wonder of engineering. To see this is to understand fully the presence of God in the world. It was God that made the fabric duct available in standard and custom colors.

Finally, beneath the forest mechanics, sinking to profound depths known to German philosophers as *das ur-grund*, are three broad layers of "stuff" alternating purple/white/red with lovely, elegant, fleeting tracers, as if the "stuff" wanted to escape as well as "found." (This is the world's *foundation*.) Except for the tracers, these layers, seen in a cross-section, are plainly in imitation of Mark Rothko's 1953 "Untitled: Purple, White, and Red."*

These final layers stretch from the forest to the horizon and beyond at a depth of, oh, let's round it off at 300 feet. From that point on, the earth is hollow. (If you bang on the "Rothko crust," as it is called, with a frying pan (ideally) or any metal object, really, it's not important (although a cast-iron sautéing pan is deeply satisfying), you will hear a hollow clanging echo from immense depths up to the length of an American football field where lies the center of the Earth, approximately. (Contrary to legend, no, the center of the Earth is not molten but merely very warm, like air circulating from an enormous hand-held hair dryer.) The Rothko crust is not part of the forest *per se*, nonetheless the forest is dependent on it. Neither is it part of the *soi-disant* "drifting" of any continental "plate." Rather, it is like a droning chord in the bases, the *lied von der Erde*, so to speak, on which the forest floats languidly, as does the flute in Debussy's *L'Apres-midi d'un faune*.

Following his brief meditation on the miracles of the natural world, Jake looked back at his companions and found that

---

* I think this is adequate evidence for the claim, made earlier in this volume, that Nature herself is all too often guilty of the imitative fallacy.

the girl had placed Rory in a sleeper hold, or in Judo a Shime-waza (絞技), a grappling hold that critically reduces or prevents either air or blood (stateside, this is called "strangling") from passing through the neck to the lungs and, in sequence, the brain.

Jake took appropriate measures with her, and they settled in for the night—"Chingé" and his prized Sharps be damned!—there among the *trees*!

42.

"One mustn't ask apple trees for oranges, France for sun, women for love, life for happiness."

—FLAUBERT

Let us pass beyond the obsession of the Reading Public with trees and return to our Minnesota scene with Suzanne standing out in front of a boulder. She is about to tell her story (as requested by Jake).

Here is the scene:

Harshly murmured the afternoon. The sky inky clouds overhung. Distant, you could see the youngsters of the village go clanking by with football cleats and helmets, purple their scarred knees, livid their eyes, steaming their breath in the formidable air. Leaving, they shouted lustily down at us words, culpable words.

This creature, young 'Zanne, stood before us like a cutout figure, a paper doll in her modest dress and apron. Not a real girl but something a child could color in, careful to stay inside the lines, with a crayon, well aware in its immature way that there never was a girl anyway.

The scene behind her was also a copy of a copy, but *what* a copy. In a wash of green and sepia and brown stood one blaze of gold from a forsythia. Splendid! But everything around it was fading and indistinct. As for her, she stood beneath an ancient beech tree, its massive arms extended in a gesture of protection for the paper girl.*

She began, "All my life I have tried to understand the meaning of the imaginary silence in which I live."

"Excuse me," I interrupted, "but what is an imaginary silence?"

Jake gave me a fierce, chastising look as if to say, "Let her tell her story."

You should know, by the way, that the whole time she spoke Jake had a romping bronco of a hard-on pushing against the thin and frayed fabric of his trousers, his first such since Fanni's sexual Armageddon. This was not one of the Marquis's speculative hard-ons. In fact, had the trousers not been so loose on him because of all the weight he'd lost on this trip, I'm quite certain the "bronco" would have burst through the fabric. So much for his earlier claims about the triviality of sex, because 'Zanne obviously turned him on. I don't know about you, but I'm starting to warm up to Jake. Unlike Percy, there can be no question now of his humanity. He's one of us.

---

* Well, as you can see, it's another tree.

43.

I am, O Anxious One. Don't you hear my voice
surging forth with all my earthly feelings?
They yearn so high, that they have sprouted wings
and whitely fly in circles round your face.

—RILKE

Freud was right to say that there is childhood sexuality, but he was wrong to assume that there is adult sexuality. Sex is where we go when we want to flee the adults. In spite of the "bronco," when Jake fell in love at first sight with 'Zanne, he was thinking as a child. He was also a child at heart when he married Fanni, even if, as we know, she had other ideas about that.

In *Totem and Taboo* Freud relates the primordial story of humanity, its deepest trauma. He tells of the son's incestuous threat, and the father's castrating expulsion of the son. The son then joins the Band of Brothers (the Brother Hoard) earlier expelled for wanting, if not their own mother, *somebody*. But the father claimed a monopoly on all of the skirts. And so, in a guilty return, the brothers proposed murder most foul. Get Daddy out of the way then we'll see what's what.

But Freud had it wrong. We don't really care if Daddy is dead; his life is punishment enough, the sodden thing. What's wrong with Freud's fable is the idea that, once expelled, the sons ever wanted to return. The father's sex is a grinding affair of rocks, like the subduction of tectonic plates. Beneath it, women groan and think to themselves, "When will this ever be over?" There is no life in it, only fate, the wrong fate. The father is always the Dead Father, the Stone Guest, Death-in-Life.

Also wrong is the idea that all of the daughters stayed in the

patriarchal fold. Many of them sympathized with the brothers, and ran away to be with them. Even the mother must have
looked on with her pale eyes and wondered what it must be like
to move beneath something less ponderous than a continental
plate. She sighed. She joined the brothers and sisters in spirit,
and sat warm and brooding in her bed awaiting their return,
waiting for the day when life could be interesting; that is, when
life could be playful freedom.

Freud could think (and think and think) Oedipus, but he
couldn't think Dionysus. That agile god popped from the side
of the father, ran, and never looked back. He was the original Gingerbread Man. "Can't catch me," but also, "Don't look
back." Joy at release, not Freudian resentment and revenge. The
brothers indulged in a great, productive flowing away.

"Dance, dance, wherever you may be, I am the Lord of the
dance!" says he.

Once we are free of the brooding father, we expose our soft
spots to each other. We whisper. We cuddle. We pet. It's a way
of saying, "There are no adults here. We are safe. Look at this!
Touch this! Kiss kids!" Thus is it written: Give up to me thy soft
spot, prepare thyself to die knowing that I am a child and will
not harm thee, and I will accompany thee as we move toward
God, the "Anxious One," toward whom we surge "with all our
earthly feelings."

But isn't this only what we call "vanilla sex"? Without the
threat of paternal violence, will some grow bored? What we call
the perverse says, "What if we let the adults join us? What if
we let Daddy—with his heavy, dark, and stinking limbs—in?"
A scary thought but thrilling. After all, what if he won't leave
after the fun is done? The adults bring the rough stuff: the ropes,
the leather, the hurting, the choking on request, the role games.
As in, "Pretend to rape me, okay? Let's see, you're my boss and

I'm working late. Put me over that table and don't hold back! Lay on, I say! Bring on the grave, the solemn, the stern and grim timber!" In this way we draw a moustache on Nobodaddy, for the perverse is the sex that exposes its soft spots not only to other children, but to the Father's Law.

But those are the odd occasions. Mostly sex is something invented by and exclusively for children, who wish to sprout wings and "whitely fly in circles" around God's face.

44.

"If a story is a skeleton structure of plot, overlaid with a felicity of thought and phrase that may be called the flesh, then the pulsing heart of the creation, the one factor that gives it life and beauty, is the imagination. But this imagination must be rightly controlled."

—FROM PLOTTO, BY WILLIAM WALLACE COOK

—after Flann O'Brien, again

"Let her tell her story!" Jake loudly insisted.

"All right," I thought, "but it's on your head. And so is that stupid ancient beech tree."

I noticed that something had happened to the lighting, there was something wrong with the sun, and a section of the sky was shaking.

THE LEGEND OF JOE DAKES

Suzanne began, "When I was a child, everything conspired in magic. Misshapen things fell out of cupboards. Even our conversations, our quarrels, to be honest, had the darkness of magic in them."

As she spoke, the western sky turned from flaming yellow to a lambent apple-green. Languorous in the air wafted the scent of syringa, which brought back, with a satisfying pain, the memory of other springs and past lives richly lived.

"My father was a major in the Army of the British Raj, mother and father of his native rifles."

God damn, there it is again, the stinking British Raj, the ridiculous Pankot rifles in their colorful Sepoy britches. This is the price I pay for letting the trees in. Apparently, the licentious child now feels she has narrative license to say anything she pleases.

"I was just a girl when he came to me to say his goodbyes before shipping off to India to join his loyal native forces. He bent down on one knee and took my two small hands in his.

"'Darling child,' he said, 'I want to tell you something before I leave, in case I don't return.'"

Her father enjoyed human frailty for its own sake.

"'You must listen carefully. One day you will meet a young man and you will marry. But you will never have any idea what he's really like. You will always be puzzled by his jokes. And then one day you will sit by his deathbed and it will seem that he is worse than a stranger—he is someone you have forgotten. Meddlesome aunts will say, "You had such a good life together," but you will hear it as a reproach.'

"Wiping a tear from my cheek, Daddy said, 'It will not matter to him whether you were there or not. He is dead and he has forgotten you in just the way that dead people do.'

"'Oh, Daddy!'

"'But at least you will have learned that you are a series of meaningless moments, always vanishing.'

"'Stop! Daddy!'"

In my time I had learned a lot about men in action, so I said, "Your father is a very wise man."

"Was. He never returned to us."

"I'm sorry to hear that. It would have given me pleasure to shake his hand."

This gave her childish heart pause. She stood still for a minute and turned a keen glance up the river into the smoky thickness of the distance, which was suddenly flushed crimson with the last purple and blood-red glow of sunset.

She continued.

"The next day Daddy decided he would not go after all. But the colonel dropped by to say, 'This is not your call.' Daddy claimed that his collection of bottles—the claret, the Madeira, the rubicund port, the single-malt, the old hock, and, for private thoughts, the special rum punch—was at risk if he left.

"'Explain yourself, man,' said Colonel Blinker Chapel.

"'It's simple: if I go Grandpa will drink it all,' he replied.

"'The devil! The devil you say!'

"'Now you understand me?'

"'I do indeed. But my dear fellow, those are the tides of war. Those the risks. I would not wait for a concrete bargain if I were you.'

"Grandpa peeked from around the door. He'd been unlucky in life. He'd placed demands on his will, given it a shot, but by teatime it was dark and he was lost. Or that's how he explained it. I was never very clear about where the tea came in. Anyway, the bottles were Daddy's last hope, especially the old hock. The idea of the old hock made him 'sanguine,' and so he wished to stay."

It was not raining, but the clouds were a level dun. Rory handed out presents, just some little things. Keepsakes, I suppose you'd call them. Perhaps magic *is* a normal part of life.

She continued. "I've seen a lot of gaiety in my noisy life, but nothing like what followed my father's departure for the Malay front. At the time, I was merely a body, sitting at a table. I had no sense of myself as a person."

"Nor should you now," I suggested. A halfhearted glare from Jake.

"As my grandfather worked his way through Daddy's bottles, he became . . . *singular*, as my aunts put it. (As in, 'Oh, dear, how very singular!') At dinnertime he would put a large cardboard box under the table. Wearing his stained boxer shorts with the cowboys on them (sent to him by an admirer in Wichita, Kansas, U.S.A.), and a bottle in his hand, he would crawl beneath the table and get in the box. Of course, we all bent under to see what he was doing. His knees poked up above the edge of the box. His head was as far down as he could manage. In-between swigs from Daddy's bottles he sang some of the old songs about the old days in the old country. One of the songs went, 'Tooraloorah something tooraloorah.' I raised up and exclaimed, 'Look at Grandpa!' But all of my aunts in their long calico dresses with the buttons in front were gone. I looked around, my eyes burning with anguish. The room turned dark. I felt grandpa's hand on my bare thigh, and I froze like a tiny, scared mouse."

At long last, some sunshine peeking out over yonder, even though the sun itself had been diminished by about a quarter. The segment of shaking sky had really done some damage. The dauntless sun clung to its pride.

Apparently, she was done. Apparently, she thought that the rest of the story told itself. The artist pushed back his Borsalino with its fine woven grasses and whistled. He blew her a kiss. Jake looked on, lovestruck. The atrocious head of his cock had now succeeded in making a small tear in his pants and was purple with the exertion, like the strong man at the circus breaking his chains. Rory was napping in the grass, an emerald ash borer making its way through his hair, looking for a place to bore, I suppose. Some more fucking sunshine. Over yonder, if you please.

45.

"The universe [started] in a smooth and ordered state and [became] lumpy and disordered as time went on."
—STEPHEN HAWKING

I'm sorry. This story is a mess. It started off well enough, long ago, but now it's lumpy gravy. It began with a strange messenger coming to a house in the middle of the night, but that's how all stories start. Then the Marquis, *Halo*, the Queen of Spells . . . that was all fine. Even Percy was okay, if you remember him. But this! I don't even know how to explain *why* it's a mess. Is it that the characters have "taken on a life of their own," as some novelists claim that theirs do, but, lamentably, my characters don't have a clue about how that might be done? Or is it that my readers (if you will allow me a hypothetical) have sensed my weakness and tried to turn my story into something more "conventional," and, being essentially stupid, are running the thing into the ground? First they had a simple request for trees. Okay. I tried to be reasonable. I guess they thought they had carte blanche after that. "How 'bout some weather?" they asked. So they stuck in some weather. The sky was a "lambent apple-green"? Have you ever seen a sky like that? And what about that three-quarter sun? At which point, perhaps, they thought, "How about a sad story?" Then comes this crazy obsession of theirs with the British Raj. And now, this dreadful memoir stuff about growing up in an alcoholic household and being sexually abused by a family member. You'd think that readers had gotten enough of that in their own lives and would like something different in a novel. And I had such high hopes for Suzanne and Jake, a regular *For Whom the Bell Tolls* of tragic romance, but you can forget that now.

Finally, sensing what a disaster they had on their hands, I think they just went for the universal plan B these days—"What about some porn?"—and threw in Jake's ridiculous boner tearing a hole in his pants. Chaste Jake! Of all people. The very soul of modesty and youthful innocence. And just how is such a thing even done? I doubt that my male readers have ever had their erections tear a hole in their clothing, and I know that they've probably had really hard ones, good as they come. If erections could tear holes in cloth, I'd trust my boyos to be the first ones to accomplish it. And this title? "The Legend of Joe Dakes"? What's that all about? Maybe they thought they could sell it to *Boy's Life*. What's next? Indian Joe?

All I can say is, *Culpam transferre in alium!*

Or perhaps it's no one's fault. Perhaps it's simply that my story has used up its energy source like a star that has exhausted its once-infinite supply of hydrogen, and now it is taking on all kinds of weird behavior: it's pulsing, losing control of its own boundaries, spinning ominously, growing hotter and hotter, and now on the cusp of exploding or collapsing, it can't quite seem to make up its mind which.

Well, if it's just a law of nature taking effect, there's not much to say about that, although this one is pretty disappointing as laws of nature go. After all, what do you say to gravity? "Stop it"? And in the end readers are their own sort of reality, a sort of parallel reality, folded into a hidden dimension like strings and their branes, where the proper laws of novel-making don't apply, as I hope the meddlers can see now. Don't you feel the opaque presence of the Reader, calmly paring His nails, now and then pointing downward and giving His awesome directives, bent brooding over the spinning world?

The immortal Gods do what they will, and I have nothing to say about that. But the characters, ah, there I think I still have some as yet unexpended and salutary authority to exercise.

You'll see. *They'll* see.

46.

"Now, children, off to bed with you! The Sandman is coming, I can already hear him."

—E.T.A. HOFFMANN

After Suzanne's weird little autobiographical tale, we were all just standing around in the clearing before her boulder. Out of nowhere, coffee and a tray of cookies appeared, as if this were a reception for the artist. The whole thing made me sick. I began to improve my coffee with some brandy that her grandfather had apparently missed during his binge. I bided my time, but it was not long before it was long enough. I made my move.

I went over to 'Zanne and removed a cup of coffee from her hand, took her cookie—a Lorna Doone, I believe, something store-bought—and threw it into my mouth, then chewed it menacingly.

I said, "Can I speak with you for just a minute? Privately."

She looked worried. She had begun to relax, and I think she had enjoyed her little moment at the center of the stage. She may even have begun to believe that we'd all been moved by her preposterous tale and felt human sympathy for her. And she'd certainly caught Jake's saucy eye—and liked what she saw there. But my only thought was that her tale now littered my tale like a kitchen garbage bag that some trailer-park refugee had tossed out the window of his '94 Chevy at 50 miles per hour scattering green-bean tins, coffee grounds, and soiled diapers on the road.

I said, "Let's just step backstage behind our fabled boulder. The great boulder from behind which you came and to which you must, as all mortal things must, return."

I knew she didn't want to go, but then I also knew she knew she didn't have a choice.

"No," she said, and I drew her on.

"No, Grandpa."

"I'm not your grandpa."

Fucking sunshine in shards that had broken the sky!

"Your face! Cartoons! It's horrible!"

And that, as they say, went too far—I stood all I could stands and I can't stands no more.

Later, a bowl of rum punch was placed in the middle of our circle. The ash borer had in fact made a little hole in Rory's head, relieving some unwanted pressure, thanks be to God. He was a different man after that.

We drank till we fell down.

47.

"Against the new masonry I re-erected the old rampart of bones. For the half of a century no mortal has disturbed them. In pace requiescat!"

—POE, "THE CASK OF AMONTILLADO"

That night, I decided that we needed a little Rory-vacation, and so I got Jake to help me put him in a gunny sack and place him in what is oft called a shallow grave. After receiving assurances from us that we'd retrieve him in the morning, he got into the bag without a struggle (the bug lobotomy probably helped to make him pliant and un-Rory-like).

Relieved of Rory's chattering presence, Jake and I were free to share the little tent and a very heart-to-heart talk. I told Jake that, frankly, I thought he was his own worst enemy, and he replied, cogently, that whether he was or not there were a number of things I needed to account for, beginning with the whereabouts (he wanted to use the word "fate" but I wouldn't let him) of his newly minted love, the specular—but oh how lovely!—Suzanne.

I beat around the bushy questions regarding the girl and pressed home questions about his mental state, until at an early hour—stupid crickets chirping morosely from every direction, cicadas like something out of Stockhausen—we began to feel drowsy.

Just before falling asleep, Jake in fact inquired about the crickets and why they seemed to be "after him." I replied that they were probably looking for me but that, in the end, they are after all of us. He asked if I could tell which way they were moving and I lied in saying that they were moving away, while in fact any moron could hear that they were practically chewing on our tent's canvas. Then, poor dear, he fell asleep leaving me alone to confront the beasts.

The next morning I dragged myself stiffly from the pup tent and was astonished to see that we had been joined overnight by many large tents. It looked either like an army encampment or a scene from a circus movie. I swear that I hadn't slept all night, so I don't know how they had set up without my hearing them, but that only tells you just how loud those crickets were!

This was the last straw. I had to act quickly before our little camp was absorbed by this army or circus and we found ourselves either running through barbed wire and dodging machine-gun fire or prancing with little dogs in dresses and hats.

"Jake! Get up! We're getting out of here!"

"What?"

"We're moving. Forget the tent, just get up and let's get started."

"What about Rory?"

"What about Rory?"

"We promised to dig him up."

"Don't be a stickler."

"So should I suppose that something like this has happened to Suzanne as well?"

"Imagine whatever you like."

He looked at me as if for the first time. He really put me under scrutiny.

"There's something about you."

"Like what?"

"Your face. It's a cartoon, isn't it? Look how you change it. Right now it's like old Prince Valiant, all innocent, handsome, and virtuous, but you don't fool me. You are an evil man, and you have done something very wrong to the woman I love. If you understand the meaning of that word."

"Which word?"

"Love."

"Of course I know that word."

"At any rate, I'm not going."

"Oh, you're going."

A half-hour later we were seated at a Denny's at a truck stop on I-39, and Jake was eating a Grand Slam breakfast while syrup sobbed off his pancakes. To appease him I'd had the cook make a Mickey Mouse pancake, with ears, etc.—he even put a little chocolate smile on it. Nevertheless, I doubt that he was really at peace with what had happened to him. I knew that he was just waiting for an opportunity to act out.

I began to wish I'd buried him too.

48.

"'Sal, we gotta go and never stop going till we get there.'
'Where we going, man?'
'I don't know but we gotta go.'"

—JACK KEROUAC

Lacking any other means of conveyance, we began our final trip home by hitchhiking. Which was fine, I wasn't above it, done plenty of it in my speckled past. I was a little worried, though, that I'd picked up some new readers who were trying to turn this into some sort of beatnik buddy film. In the early afternoon, barely ten miles into our journey, we found ourselves on a remote country road on which no car passed us in either direction for several hours. I was angry (as I always am when the objective world refuses to be a direct expression of my will, which means that I am—like my tragic friend back on Islay—always angry to some degree). Jake, though, had found some mindless satisfaction creating mosaics in the dirt with tiny pebbles (pea gravel) left over from the last chip-and-seal job by the county road crew. Quickly, one after the next, he arranged the little rounded rocks to look like his great love, Suzanne. And I don't think a photographer could have done a more lifelike job. His portrait of her was amazingly detailed, black-and-white photorealism done with little worthless pebbles, a real work of art.

Just before I scattered his pebbles with my foot, I said, "That's quite good, Jake. You have a real knack for whatever you'd call what you're doing." Swoosh, rackety-rock and clatter-away. He didn't even bother to look up at me, wouldn't give me the satisfaction. He just started re-creating the mosaic of his beloved.

So there we sat. At last I saw, in the distance, a large automobile approaching slowly from the north. It couldn't have been doing much more than a few miles an hour, barely crawling, as if its purpose were to annoy me. At last it stopped before us, like some hulking ghost ship without a crew. It was a '63 Buick LeSabre convertible in good, if dirty, condition. I looked inside, and there, sure enough, was Rory.

He lowered the passenger-side window and peered at me. "Need a ride?"

"Well, of course I need a ride. But I thought I left you back at camp buried in a shallow grave."

He frowned. "Yes, you did, but only once, and I'm trying not to hold it against you."

"Look, Rory, I'm sorry about that, but it was merely personal. I mean, I didn't bury you out of principle, and I wasn't doing my job, and I wasn't following orders. I was simply trying to get rid of you because I don't like you. I'm sorry to have to put it that way."

"I appreciate your honesty."

"So, how did you get here, on this particular highway, in this car, of all cars?"

He reached across and opened the passenger door.

"Get in."

"Is it safe? You really know how to drive? And you promise you're not angry?"

"Does it matter?"

He had me there. So I stepped back and pulled Jake up from

the dirt. (Frankly, if we'd just left him there, I don't think he'd have cared. He seemed happy enough with the pebbles and his artistic pursuits.) I put him in the backseat, where he sat stupe-fied, although even that probably gives him too much credit. At any rate, he was in the backseat. Unless his hair catches fire, ignore him.

I got in beside Rory and slammed the massive Buick door shut.

"Now," I said, "you were going to tell me how you happened to be here."

Rory stared at me for a moment, as if he were trying to put my face together, as if it had a bad case of Brownian motion. He was trying to "fix" me, like a drunk trying to get his wife's face to stop spinning.

"I've never noticed this before, but you have a cartoon face."

"Not this nonsense again! Rocky? Bullwinkle?"

"I think it's Archie, but it keeps changing."

"Good grief. At least it's not Veronica, or Bizzaro!"

Then, looking forward, Rory put the car in gear and started off, again at something well under the speed limit, unless it was yet another example of time dilation and we merely seemed to be going slowly from some perspective outside the car, if that's how that bit of science is supposed to work.

"Are you going to tell me?"

Nothing.

"Is this as fast as this thing goes?"

Nothing.

I felt like I was prodding a pulpy bug that was lethargic with the approach of winter.

A few minutes passed before he said, "What?"

"Are you going to tell me why you're here?"

"I don't remember saying that I was going to tell you why I'm here. Besides, you wouldn't understand."

"Try me."

"How about if I give you the simple version?"

"We can start there."

"I'm here because this is the world in which you can ask me why I'm here."

"That's the simple version?"

"I warned you."

"Can you explain what you mean?"

"It will hurt."

"More than this?"

"Okay, then. While I'm here now with you, in this time and this place, every other possibility is playing itself out. You're on a different road, every possible road. The car is a different car, every possible car—a Dodge Sierra station wagon, a Rambler, a Ford Pinto on fire, or your mother's old Plymouth. And we are every possible version of ourselves. (Plus or minus a three-percent allowance for sampling error.) Those are just the big variables. Now multiply them out. There is an equation, if you think that might help."

"I hate equations, but your sentences are not much help either."

"Okay, so,

$$\delta s = \delta \int_{t_1}^{t_2} L(q, \dot{q}, t)dt = 0$$

or something close to that."

"Oh, come on, that can't be right. That is a basic principle of classical mechanics where S is the action, the integral of the Lagrangian multiplier determining the local maxima and minima of a function subject to equality constraints."

Rory looked like I'd hurt his feelings.

"I paid a lot of money for that equation. It's very high-end," he said.

"What's that got to do with it?"

"Okay, let me try again. I'll make it simple so you'll understand. Take R, where R is reality, and ∞, which is, as always, our old friend infinity."

"He's no friend of mine."

"Now the equation.

"$R = roads/\infty \times car/\infty \times you/\infty \times me/\infty \times \infty/\infty$ and all that divided by C^2. I hope it doesn't disappoint you that it's just another inverse square equation. But that's important because without it there wouldn't be anything to hold it all together. In other words, the equation requires an acknowledgment of gravity."

"I notice that it didn't include an acknowledgment of Jake."

He looked back.

"Would you acknowledge Jake?"

"Agreed. Agreed."

"Actually, it just happens that in this world Jake is in a coma-like state in the backseat—in this case this backseat, in other cases other backseats. Are you starting to get it? In others he's in his "steady state," and every other possible state of Jakeness, including one that I'm particularly fond of in which a Roy Orbison–like Jake sings 'Blue Bayou.'"

"That song always makes me cry. Feel so bad I've got a worried mind."

"There is one other possibility that I ought to alert you to. It is possible that he is not in a coma-like state at all. It could be that he himself *is* the cosmological constant."

"???"

"In short, Jake could be the very thing that Einstein sought: the cosmological principle that makes the universe eternal rather than doomed to infinite expansion into the inky depths of space."

"We're trusting *Jake* with this?"

"If I'm right, Jake's hair should catch fire shortly."

Then a thought struck me.

"Doesn't . . . ," I asked, "Doesn't . . . "

He completed my thought, "Doesn't that mean that our campground this morning was the functional equivalent of the Big Bang?"

I sighed in relief. "Yes!"

"True, but I wouldn't take that homely fact too seriously. Campgrounds are exploding at this very moment in every corner of our universe. Billions and billions of them."

I'm dazzled by this vision.

"You mean, campground supernovas exploding in tents and sleeping bags and freeze-dried turkey tetrazzini and marshmallows and Coleman lanterns and more marshmallows and martinis and first-grade report cards and whoosh! a covered wagon and Indians to chase it and there goes the first girl you ever kissed, her lips still puckered, and now the corn crib you kissed her behind, then ceramic elephants, croquet bats, and badminton nets with baseball gloves signed by Orlando Cepeda entwined, and Labrador retrievers, televisions, pachucos with their hair greased back, a copy of *The Last of the Mohicans,* guinea pigs in pockets, a pack of Lucky Strikes, a bale of dog money, and everything you have, every what have you, all flowing out of the campground and out across the universe. This is marvelous! Science is not only true, it's charming!"

Rory looked at me sternly.

"You may have noticed that God is nowhere to be found in this."

"I *did,* you scoundrel."

"I think this bears on the behavior of some people we know, not naming any names."

He meant the Marquis, I believe. Just a hunch.

"Note this well: it is easy to act as if God does not exist," he looked at me intently, and pointed at me, fixing my attention, "but it is much worse in this case, with the person in question, because it would appear that *he is sincere!* And that is unforgivable."

"And until this unnamed man, by whom we of course mean your former employer, until he came along with his dirty ermine sleeves and his blasted sincerity, we had all been *kidding* about there being no God?"

"Exactly."

Just then, Rory reached into the glove compartment and pulled out the Smith and Wesson .38, as mysteriously returned to this adventure as Rory himself.

49.

"Nobody ever gets anything right. That is the human condition, and there is no value in fretting over it."

—MORSE PECKHAM

Even at 20 miles per hour in a '63 Buick LeSabre, you eventually get to where you're going. As we approached the Marquis's château, I couldn't help feeling a little nostalgic tug at my heart.

The memories!

Pulling into the circular drive, I noticed that the grounds had not been tended in many weeks. The grass was long and brown; dandelions and chickweed flourished. Nearer the house Afghan Love and Hempstar diesel, a particularly vigorous cultivar with sky-high THC content, climbed the walls, their bright-green and serrated leaves lush and thick.

I looked round to the backseat to see if Jake was still with us. I was amazed at what I saw. Not only was Jake there, vividly there, but he had a protective arm around the hunched shoulders of Suzanne! She was shivering beneath a wool blanket, army surplus, the kind of stuff that Allied ski troops froze beneath in the Apennines during the last months of World War II. Her hair was wet and hung in ropy braids slick and stiff with mud. She looked like Millais's Ophelia dragged from her mossy pond. Jake shot me a resentful tough-if-you-don't-like-it look. I think he cordially hated my guts at that moment.

Believe it or not, I was okay with this. I thought, "Well, I'll be damned! The two youngsters really care for each other." Besides, I had other problems just then.

"My God," said Rory, looking toward the weed-choked château, "I hope His Excellence is okay."

Don't misunderstand this sentiment. He was only worried that he wouldn't be able to shoot him.

"He's having the time of his life," I said, "just look at the porch."

On the wide porch, three burly security men sat in rocking chairs, assault rifles across their laps, and fat spliffs hanging from their lips.

"Looks like he's moved on from the craft brews," said Rory, opining. "Impressive. I wonder where he found the Navy SEALs."

I yelled out to them, "Hi! We come in peace. Would like to talk to your leader."

Nothing. They didn't even move. But then out of nowhere a voice: "Hands where we can see semen!"

Slowly, we got out of the Buick and walked toward the house, our hands up and open.

"Hands where we can semen . . . !"

I turned to my confreres, "Did that Ranger just say 'semen'?"

Jake dropped his hands and said, "Dummies."

"What?"

"*Dummies.*"

Just then the Marquis stuck his head out from behind the front door.

"Jake!" he cried.

"Grandpa!"

Rory ran toward the Marquis.

"Sir, it's so wonderful to see you, so wonderful to be home!"

Rory had fallen quickly from his Masters of the Universe know-it-all state back to his default condition of servile and witless toady. The Marquis rebuffed him deftly with a dowdy ermine swish of his tatty purple sleeve.

Frowning, he said to us, "Our bursar informed me last month that I was a squatter. In my own boyhood home! Squatting! An ugly word with unpleasant connotations. They say I'll be evicted, but my public defender has resisted. He says that the term 'squatting' is not acceptable to the defense, but if they can come up with a different word I'll leave voluntarily. Apparently they're still working on it, thank God. Apparently, they don't have a thesaurus."

He looked at us and beamed. Gesturing toward the Rangers, he said, "Don't mind them. I think their batteries are running low." Then throwing open his arms, "Come to papa!"

But for some reason Jake was diffident. Perhaps he was worried that the Marquis would be angry because he was still without employment.

So the Marquis continued, speaking harshly toward Rory, "It goes without saying that I am bankrupt. As a consequence, the bursar fired you, Rory. I saw him check the box. Rory ☑ *terminado*. At least he said he was my bursar, although it's possible he was just one of those Mexican boys who used to cut the lawn. But what do lawn boys know of bursting, or whatever it is that a bursar does? In any case, your hugs mean nothing to me now."

"Sir!"

"Besides, as you can see, I am keeping different company these days."

"You mean these crash-test dummies?" I asked.

"I can no longer afford to employ my rotating team of security peasants."

"Rotating peasants?" I queried.

The Marquis looked at me suspiciously.

"Who is this fellow? I don't much care for his attitude. And what's the matter with his face? He reminds me of Mortimer Snerd."

"I beg your pardon!"

"Beg all you like. As a member of the landed gentry, I'm well used to beggars. Anyway, these fellows—'dummies,' as you crudely put it—are much better than the peasants. They are *industry standard*." He winked stupidly. "That's all I should need to say, but that's probably asking a lot of you. See if this helps: they meet all *best practices*. Every one of them. They are personal security with enhancements."

He pulled a pamphlet from an inner pocket of his robe.

"Here, Rory, read this, will you?"

Rory reads: "Glockman™ is a life-size simulated male that appears to be six feet tall and one hundred-eighty lean athletic pounds. He provides the impression of a highly trained guard. He is a unique security product with movable latex head and hands."

"I dress him according to my own sense of style," continued the Marquis, "the ball cap, the mirror shades, the copy of *The Sporting News*, and the button-on legs complete a powerful visual effect. Don't you agree? I even got the optional zippered carrying tote for discrete portability so that at least one of my boys can come with me on vacations. I've become very fond of them."

Rory, reading the pamphlet, "Says here that sex parts are available in three sizes."

The Marquis put his arms akimbo, looked down his nose grinning, and said, "Now, Rory, you know I don't roll like that. And that is not in the brochure. You're being peevish and just maybe a little jealous. Would it help if I said that I'm sorry the bursar fired you?"

"I see that you didn't pay for button-on legs for everybody," I volunteered.

"No. But they don't mind sharing," he paused. "But you miss the fact that each is augmented in a way that makes legs superfluous. Those sunglasses they wear are more than mere sunglasses. They are equipped with MEG 4.0 ultra-compact wearable display devices, a peripheral treatment for Web-based but head-mounted eyewear. In short, they can browse the Web on their glasses. I've ordered the contact-lens version, the one with the bionanotechnology, but they're on back order. I'm told that I'm in the first thirty million scheduled for order fulfillment, so it won't be long. In any event, these boys are ready for whatever comes at them. A home invader will never know if Glockman is simply looking him over, doing a background check through INTERPOL, calling in air support, or watching a Latina she-male tearing up a MILF on PornFace."

Jake looked worried. He peered at his grandfather as an astronomer peers at a fuzzy patch that he hopes is a coherent galaxy but fears is just another nebulous jumble of space dust.

"But Grandpa, these are latex. They're dummies. They can't actually see."

The Marquis looked a little flustered at first, but he pulled himself together.

"First, I have known my share of dummies, and they are not limited to latex people. Second, do you have any idea how hard it is to live with nothing more to look forward to than the extermination of an eternal flood of digital aliens? It's like living in order to kill cockroaches with wooden spoons. That's nobody's idea of a purpose-driven life, not even mine."

The Marquis began to cry with frustration and loneliness, but I was not deceived. I knew his wickedness. He cried only to deceive us. All I saw in his tears was the great baby, the world, that had tormented itself for the last 4.543 billion years.

"These lads," he gestured at the Glockmen, "have brought me kindness and the common touch."

The Marquis looked like he was dissolving, one cell at a time, some vile essence in a puddle at his feet.

"I was so very, very alone," he pled.

Kindly, Suzanne spoke up from beneath her blanket. She was visibly moved by this emotionally extortionate spectacle. She had every appearance of being compassionate, and she probably was a compassionate person, but she might have been trying to make me feel guilty about bludgeoning her with a rock and dumping her in a lake.

"They look nice to me! Where did you get your companions, Your Majesty?" she said, softly, her eyes nurturing.

"Oh, Jake, you haven't introduced me to your lovely if sopping friend. And please, call me Grandpa."

She smiled. Jake smiled. Everybody smiled. He could be charming.

"And I'm glad you asked, young lady. It's a curious story of the sort I never thought I'd live to see but, then, here it is. Well, one day—before my cellphone was disconnected—I was called by the nice people at Mass Platform, Basalt Cliffs, and Fringing-Reef Tectronics. They wanted me to know that as one of their very best customers I was eligible to buy a security system from them. You know, one of the marvels of these times is how easy it is to be a customer. And I did need a new security system, since my loyal peasant squads had been vanquished from the land, so I ordered one.

"Well, you know how they work, once I had the Basic System they wanted to sell me the rest. I was offered my own Predator drone aircraft that I could command from my iPhone. Knowing me as you do, you won't be surprised to hear that this was an exciting opportunity for me. Thanks to the Xbox, I can operate any form of remote thingee. I mean, I can make that shit hum. Unfortunately, I could only get enough credit from them to get the community-outreach software that provides coverage limited to the local zip code. I was disappointed. Sure, I could call in rounds on a few local towns, and the idea of blowing up Towanda had its appeal. Still, what they offered at this low, low introductory price was a lot better than nothing and no doubt adequate for policing the lower orders in the neighborhood."

Amused, I asked, "And where are the missiles?"

He nearly hopped in his excitement, clapping his hands like Ed Wynn.

"Oh, we don't need our own missiles. We *virtually* own, say, two launches per contract period, but the actual missiles we share with other subscribers while Mass Platform maintains the arsenal.

"Of course, a little skepticism was no doubt in order, so once the software was downloaded to my laptop I burned one of my missiles for the month and destroyed my own garden shed."

He pointed to the west of the château.

"And as you can see, it is bloody well gone, and that includes that damned green riding mower."

All I could see was a featureless field of weeds and, of course, the artist with his easel, painting away. I caught his eye and he doffed his Borsalino to me, smiling gently.

"But I was lucky to get even that shot off. The sheriff sent a man by to say that I couldn't launch another until I had a license for concealed carry. Details! He put a block on my launch security code. Must've been a clause in the fine print, or the sweet man from Mumbai neglected to explain the license when he sold me the service over the phone."

"Who else has these things?"

"Ah," he laughed, "that's the rub, isn't it? In theory, anyone can have the contract, anyone can have a Predator, and so it would be careless if I didn't assume that everyone *does* have one and can fire a missile at will. Even the homeless have cellphones and so could, in theory, take down anyone foolish enough not to throw folding money into their outstretched caps. Imagine, a high-tech protection racket run out of a homeless shelter! That's a sign of the times.

"However, through our Neighborhood Watch Association we have negotiated an agreement and have declared sanity." He laughed. "For all the good that does anyone."

Now he practically leered, bent at the waist, hands on his knees, chest heaving, like he was having a heart attack.

"I hope you see the larger irony. We do not each have a Predator at our disposal. We don't even have a missile on a Predator. The system, as the company readily admits, is over-subscribed.

Their perfectly legal and perfectly legitimate assumption is that there will never be a time when everyone wants to scramble a drone and launch a missile on the same day. That's covered in the war-of-all-against-all exclusionary clause. They're quite upfront about it. It's just like a bank assuming that there will never be a time when everyone wants all of their money on the same day.

"There are two drones designated for local usage, and maybe a half-dozen missiles total, although even those rotate in and out of maintenance. The only thing required by the Federal Consumer Munitions Agency is that the service contract specify compensation for missile or drone non-availability, usually nothing more than ten dollars off of your next AK."

"So," I suggested, "your neighborhood is a group of people all of whom imagine that they have instant access to a devastating weapon, but the truth is that they're more like people seated in a circle with a single gun resting in the middle of the floor. A voice says, 'You do not need the gun,' and they all throw themselves at it. Is that it?"

The Marquis beamed at me.

"You are much brighter than your Donald Duck face suggests."

This was all very amusing, but Jake was getting worried at the mental frenzy of Grandpa's stories. "But what about the security dummies, Grandpa? You were going to tell us about the security dummies."

The Marquis turned to Jake, a look of profound introspection on his face.

At last he said, "I have heard it affirmed by not un-philanthropic persons, that it were a real increase of human happiness could all young men from the age of nineteen to thirty-one be covered under barrels."

Jake was mystified. Suzanne burst into tears. Were we watching as our dear friend the Marquis, with whom we'd been through so much, suffered a stroke? Were all of these thoughts leaking from a damaged mind?

No one spoke, but the Marquis replied anyway: "What?"

We looked at each other, uncertain what he could mean.

Then again, his face twisted and contorted, coming apart, as if it were being pulsed in a food processor. Then again he said, "Whaaaat?"

With that last "what?" Rory met his limit. He pulled the .38 from the small of his back and leveled it . . . at me!

Like a planet that has calmly circled its familiar sun for billions of years but whose bright eternity is ruined when it realizes that it is dependent upon magnetic fields and gravity, and, not understanding the laws of gravitational force, ceases to believe in its own possibility, thinking, "And all this time I believed that I circled the sun because it loved me." Meanwhile, it plunges sadly off toward the universe's empty regions, a fine China plate spinning away. So it was with our company of friends when they heard the Marquis say, "What?" They realized that their drama, they themselves, this entire world was not possible, and they were ashamed of it and the poor, selfish roles they had played in what was only yet another cock-and-bull story.

So Rory dropped his gun, and Suzanne dropped her blanket (woo-hoo!), and the artist dropped his brush, and Jake dropped beautiful, plangent 'Zanne's modest hand, and then everyone just stopped. In their eyes there was a moment of fear, a brief moment of peace, and then, as if they had been stricken by mass contagion, they collapsed like the puppets they were, like children in a garden game: All Fall Down.

Ashes! Ashes!

It was really very sad to see: their faces sinking, shoulders slumped, eyes burning with tears, flesh flowing a little lava-like. I already felt the lack of my characters. I missed them. It was very tempting to sit with them, throw my hands in the air, and give up. But I also knew that this had to happen and that this was how it had to be.

At last, I thought, *Consumatum est.*